Full Figured 8:

Carl Weber Presents

Full Figured 8:

Carl Weber Presents

Skyy and **Treasure Hernandez**

www.urbanbooks.net

Urban Books, LLC
97 N18th Street
Wyandanch, NY 11798

ISBN 13: 978-1-60162-406-2
ISBN 10: 1-60162-406-9

First Trade Paperback Printing August 2014
Printed in the United States of America

10 9 8 7 6 5 4 3 2 1

Distributed by Kensington Publishing Corp.
Submit Wholesale Orders to:
Kensington Publishing Corp.
C/O Penguin Group (USA) Inc.
Attention: Order Processing
405 Murray Hill Parkway
East Rutherford, NJ 07073-2316
Phone: 1-800-526-0275
Fax: 1-800-227-9604

A Lover's Embrace?

by

Skyy

Chapter 1

Hands.

I could feel hands upon my body. They made their way from the bottom of my feet up my legs stopping at my stomach. The massive hands roamed around my mounds of flesh becoming familiar with my body as if they had explored my body before. They gripped my side pulling me close to them; I could feel the body against me, yet, I could not see who it was. All I knew was the hands were strong, stronger than any hands that had touched me in years, and for once I didn't care that I was being touched in areas that I usually considered off-limits.

I woke up from my slumber, body shivering from the intensity of my dream. I hadn't wanted sex so bad since I went through my initial withdrawal period after my ex, almost five years ago. I needed a release. I got out of my bed, pulled open my dresser drawer and then rustled through the clothes until finding a small black box. I opened the box to find the only girlfriend I had known in years. I pressed the on button and my little silver friend began to vibrate in my hand. I rushed back to my bed; my body was in need of release. I lay on my back pressing my little silver girlfriend against my swollen clit. I pressed the little arrow on the control until achieving my favorite speed and pulsation allowing the vibrations to consume my body. I moved the bullet in a circular motion feeling my own wetness on my hand.

I closed my eyes and thought about the strong hands. I pressed against my clit harder. I needed more. I needed more; it felt good but I wanted something more intense. I turned over on my stomach pressing my pussy against my mattress. I turned the bullet on full blast holding on to my pillow as I ground my body against my silver girlfriend. I bit my lip and closed my eyes. I could feel the hands on me again, grabbing me with an unfamiliar roughness. I pushed my hand underneath my body pushing the bullet as far into me as I could. I ground it with intensity; my body jerked with each strong vibration.

My orgasm was rising from my toes, creeping all the way through my body. I continued to grind, my body now jerking more than ever. I moaned as the intense orgasm reached the pit of my stomach. This was going to be an epic explosion my body needed more than ever. It was so close. My body began to jerk harder and harder, until the maximum pleasure was upon me. My legs began to tremble, switching in anticipation. I was ready, my body was ready, and it wanted it more than ever. Intensity took over my body causing one giant jerk. I gasped.

Everything stopped. The vibration was gone. I turned over and looked at the controller; the lights were still on, yet, I had no vibe. Suddenly the cord felt loose. I pulled the cord but the silver bullet remained lodged inside my walls. My mouth dropped open as I stared at the dangling small wires that were once attached to my beloved electronic lover.

"No, no. No!" I panicked as I attempted to push the wires back in the end of my bullet as if it had simply come unplugged. I frantically scanned the room with my eyes for something that could either fix my bullet or take its place for the final moments in the game. I was out of luck. I wanted to cry as I could feel my orgasm creeping back inside as I stared at the pathetic remains of my now-dead girlfriend. Just like my last real girlfriend, my bullet had left me heated and unfulfilled. I wanted to scream. I threw a small temper tantrum on my bed hitting my hands against my mattress. I thought about using my own fingers but I knew it wouldn't be the same. I was never good at pleasuring myself. My stomach always seemed to get in the way whenever I tried.

I let out a deep sigh and got out of my bed and headed down my long walkway toward my studio. The cold concrete floor took away remains of the orgasm I never had.

I suddenly felt inspired. I grabbed the mound of my sculpting clay, grabbed my knife, and began to let my memory guide my hands. The cold wet clay began to take form as I shaped a torso with a round belly. I formed curves on the sides familiar to the curves I tried to hide with my Spanx daily. I closed my eyes and thought about those hands. I couldn't get the hands out of my mind. My mind guided my hands as I sculpted the image.

I looked over at the clock; three hours had passed before I had even known it. I took a step back from my work admiring my new creation. Something struck me as odd. I looked over at two of my other sculptures; the hands were very different. On my others my hands were soft, delicate, slender, and smooth. I glanced back at my new creation. These hands were different. They were strong, larger than normal, and there was nothing delicate about them. I stood there staring at my own body and clay form. These hands were definitely not the hands I was used to over my years of dating. These hands were masculine.

Chapter 2

My alarm clock freaked me out. I jumped up; my head pounded from the quick movement. I grabbed the alarm clock pulling it from the wall, throwing it with force until it crashed against my walls. I fell back on my pillow, putting my hand against my head. After my own snooze session I finally mustered the courage to get out of my bed.

I took a long, hot shower and threw on the first outfit I could find in my newly washed pile of clothes. I brushed my long, thick hair, pulling it back into a ponytail. I applied some edge control to my edges, hoping they would stay in place for at least half the day. I looked at myself in the mirror and frowned. I pulled my hair out of the ponytail, grabbed a headband, and put it on my head. I brushed my hair letting it fall down on my shoulders. I shrugged my shoulders; this look was going to have to do for the day.

I rushed back into my bedroom to grab my cordless phone that was ringing. I knew it had to be one of two people, as no one ever called my home phone. I smiled when I saw the strange number appear on the screen.

"Kev!" I squealed.

"What's up, chick?" My best friend Kevin's deep baritone voice echoed through the phone. I hadn't spoken to him in over a month.

"I should be mad at you but I'm not going to be," I pouted.

"Sorry, sweets, you already know the business."

My smile covered my face. It had been over a year since I'd seen my best friend who had taken a job as a travel photographer with the Travel Channel. Kevin and I had been best friends since the sixth grade. While I focused on my art he focused on his, photography, becoming an amazing photographer. He took his dream job shooting for the Travel Channel, which kept him out on assignments all over the world. Over the years he had become more of a big brother to me than a friend.

"It would be nice if my best friend could stop traveling the globe long enough to come and see his best friend, especially with my opening coming up."

"I am trying, Rayne. I am hoping I don't have to be in Australia then. I'm just waiting to hear from my boss."

"Well you need to tell your boss—"

Before I could finish Kevin cut me off. "I need to tell my boss that my friend doesn't care about my job if it comes in between her exhibits."

I sat silent as he attempted to mock me with a high-pitched voice. I walked into my studio and paused. There stood my creation from the night before. The big hands perplexed me. What made me create them or even dream about them.

"Kevin, I had the strangest dream last night." I continued to study the hands I created in clay.

"Uh-oh, you been eating crazy food before going to sleep again?" Kevin laughed.

His smart remark took my attention off of the sculpted hands. "No, but it was still odd."

"Rayne, babes, I gotta run. Can we pick this up at a later time?"

"Only if you promise to really try to come to my opening." I held the phone in anticipation of the response. I heard Kevin let out a loud moan.

"I promise I will do all that I can to make it to your opening. I'll call you later."

The phone hung up before I could give him a harder time. I looked at the clock sitting on my art table. I would have to think of the mysterious hands at a later time. I knew I couldn't be late for work again, or my boss would also be up my ass. I grabbed a Pop-Tart and an individual-size bottle of orange juice and headed out the door.

I walked into my office with my usual attitude, unhappy with the parking spot I landed about a mile away from the building. The large call center was buzzing as usual. I walked past the different sections from customer service to billing until making my way to the back of the building where my department resided.

"What's up, Jack?" I greeted one of my coworkers as he walked past me.

"Sup, Rayne? Having a good day so far?" Jack gave me a high five as he walked backward to try to talk to me.

"It could be better." I continued to walk as Jack disappeared.

I did my usual and headed over to my friend's desk. I sat in the empty chair as Camille finished on a call with the customer. I wanted to laugh at the fake, proper accent she was using with the customer.

"Thank you for calling and have a lovely day." Camille smiled as the customer finally hung up. She pulled her headset off and threw it on her desk.

"Wuz up, bitch?" She leaned back on her desk as she greeted me in her normal voice.

"Nothing much." I picked up a magazine off of her desk. "How is the day going?"

Camille rolled her eyes. "Girl, bullshit is usual. What you been up to this morning? From the looks of that outfit you must have spent the whole night working again."

"Something like that."

We both turned around as we noticed a line of people coming from the training room. We watched as the new hires started to look around for their new desks.

"Shit I forgot they start today." Camille rolled her eyes again. "I know they bet not ask me nothing today. I am not in the mood."

Just then one of the new hires walked over to us. "Hi, um . . ." she stuttered.

I looked at the desk and noticed the new nametag that was pinned on the wall. "Oh, I'm sorry," I said as I stood up, pushing the chair back to her new desk. "I'm just sitting here in your seat."

"It's okay." The girl smiled. She was a cute, brown-skinned natural female. Her twist out was better than many that I'd seen around the office. It was obvious she had been natural for quite some time.

"My name is Rayne and this is your neighbor, Camille. She's one of the best so any questions make sure to ask her." I smiled. I knew Camille wanted to slap me for volunteering her services. I winked as Camille threw her middle finger up at me as I walked away.

I made my way over to my cubicle bay area. I greeted my other coworkers as they sat back watching the new hires settling into their desks. Janice and Rosalyn both couldn't take their eyes off the far side of our section. They were two of the older workers who had been there for years and they made sure everyone knew it.

"Hi, Rayne; it's new hire day." It had only taken me about a month to get use to Rosalyn's thick Spanish accent. She smiled at me as she peeled an orange.

"I guess." I put my bag on my desk and sat down in my chair. "So who do we have over here?" I looked at the nametag on the desk next to mine. "Loyal Santos; are we getting a new Spanish rep?"

The frown on Rosalyn's face let me know the thought of a new Spanish agent didn't sit well with her.

"I didn't hear we were getting a new one," Janice chimed in as she pulled her reading glasses off.

"What kind of name is Loyal?" I frowned as I sat in my seat.

Between Janice and Rosalyn I knew anything and everything that happened in our call center. They were like the two gossiping women who never admitted to actually gossiping. I had grown used to them over the last year of being in my department. If nothing else they kept me laughing, and kept the normal drama of call centers away from our area. I never quite understood how they knew everything, yet never were seen talking to anyone outside of our little area. They both also knew every way to work the system. They schooled to programs like FMLA, which had become a godsend since I started working on my piece for my exhibit.

"Well we don't need another Spanish agent; I don't get that many calls as is," Rosalyn added just as her phone began to ring. Instantly she was speaking Spanish to the caller.

"Loyal," Janice grunted. "You know I never trust people with names like that. You know, Loyal, Cherish, Angel, Patience, Precious; usually folks with those names are polar opposites of whatever their name actually means. Angels be more like Devils."

We all laughed.

I turned my computer on and prepared to start the day. While my computer started up, I headed over to the coffeemaker to find it empty as usual. I couldn't understand why so many people drank the coffee but never thought to start a new batch when they drank the last. I opened the door only to see a canister of Folgers almost completely empty. I walked back over to my desk and opened my bottom drawer where I kept all of my special goodies. I pulled out a bag of vanilla Starbucks and headed back to the coffeemaker. Within moments the aroma filled the air causing some of the main coffee drinkers' heads to pop up from their cubicles.

"That smells amazing," an unfamiliar male voice said behind me.

I turned around to find an unfamiliar face to match the voice. He smiled. He was very polished, more than most of the men who worked in my department. His head was bald and very smooth. There wasn't a trace of a hair follicle to be found on his head. He had a beard that was also lined perfectly with just enough hair to create the beard, nothing hanging down off of his face. His skin was a peculiar shade of brown, almost the same as a coffee with cream in it.

"Would you like some?" I held a cup out to him.

"Really? Thank you that would be wonderful. I'll come and get it after I put my things down at my desk." He smiled. He had a great smile to match the rest of his appearance.

I let the coffee finish percolating, poured me a cup, and headed back to my desk. I stopped in my tracks when I saw the same guy settling into the desk connected to mine. I glanced at the look on Janice's face. She was smiling harder than I had ever seen before. I noticed two of the other older women in my section also staring at the new eye candy. I couldn't help but laugh to myself. This was going to be very interesting.

"Rayne, did you meet Loyal?" Janice extended her hand to present him.

"We met briefly at the coffeemaker." He smiled at me again.

I didn't know why I suddenly felt uneasy. I sat down at my desk and turned around to my computer.

I stared at the computer screen as Janice and Rosalyn got to know our new associate. It didn't take long to find out he was forty-two, had one son, recently moved back to Memphis from living in St. Louis for the last few years and, of course, was single. I couldn't help but laugh at the not-so-subtle flirting from Janice, who used her age as her excuse to say whatever she wanted to say.

I pulled my art pad and pencil set out. The images from the night before were still etched in my brain. I began to sketch the sculpture I started working on the night before. I was still fixated on the hands. I didn't know why I wanted to get them right. Before I knew it my break time finally had come.

"And who is this?"

I turned around when I heard Mrs. Loretta's raspy voice headed in our direction. The four foot eight inch woman sashayed over to Janice's desk putting her skinny arm on Janice's shoulder.

"Hello, I'm Loyal."

I shook my head as he flashed his smile to the wrong person. Ms. Loretta perked up instantly.

"Loyal, huh?" Ms. Loretta looked him up and down. "You sure are a cutie pie."

"Down, Loretta." Janice laughed.

"How old are you, chile?" Ms. Loretta pushed her reading glasses up on her nose.

"I'm forty-two."

Loretta waved him off with her hand. "Oh you just a baby."

"I wouldn't say all that." He smiled again.

"Chile, please, what can I do with a forty-year-old?" Ms. Loretta shook her head.

"Woman, who said he wanted you to do anything, hell even think anything?" Janice joked back. "You better shut up before I tell your husband."

Ms. Loretta frowned at Janice. They all laughed. He had a distinctive laugh that echoed in our little area.

"Please ain't nothing wrong with looking." Ms. Loretta playfully put her hand on Loyal's left bicep. "Oh, Lord, and he got muscles, too. Let me get away from this man before I end up divorced and in HR. Rayne, girl, did you meet Loyal?"

I knew what the sly smile on Ms. Loretta's face meant. She had moved on from herself to trying to fix me up. I loved the older women in my office but none would accept that I was gay, or that I was perfectly okay being single for as long as I had been.

The truth was I had been single for longer than normal. I was coming up on five years since my last relationship exploded in my face. I didn't expect to stay single for so long, but after finding my silver girlfriend I didn't have a need for a physical one. I was able to focus on me and my art, which was more important than another useless relationship.

"Yes, Ms. Loretta, we met."

"I can tell she's the quiet one." Loyal stared at me.

I felt uneasy again. I stood up.

"She's not quiet, just give her time," Janice added. "She's the life of the party."

"Riiggghhttt." I laughed as I walked away from the hen party.

I made my way back over to Camille's desk. I didn't know how any work was getting done by the laughter coming from her bay area.

"What are you guys laughing about?" I stood next to her desk.

"Girl, nothing." Camille looked at me. "So you got that new dude everyone is lusting over in your bay?"

"I guess." I leaned against her wall. "Ms. Loretta and Janice are lusting over him."

Camille laughed. "They would sit him next to your gay ass. Probably for the best. I hear he's got these chicks all open and shit."

"Again, I guess." I rolled my eyes.

I headed back to my desk. I was eager to get the day over with. I had real work to get back to at my place, and mysterious hands to complete.

Chapter 3

My eyes were heavier than normal. I kept dozing off at my desk without realizing it. I knew I couldn't continue with the long nights. I was spending my nights working on my projects and only getting a few hours of sleep.

I felt a tap on my shoulder. I turned to see Loyal holding a bottle of 5-Hour Energy and a Red Bull. "I figured you needed something and since I didn't know which you would like I figured I'd let you pick your poison."

"Thanks." I sat up in my chair and took the 5-Hour Energy from him and quickly downed the shot. "Was I that obvious?"

"Naa, no snoring or anything." Loyal smiled. He did have a cute smile.

I looked at the clock. The day was going fast. We were the only late shift of people in our department. Our supervisor and other coworkers had already gone home for the night. I liked it when everyone left. The calls would slow down and it was quiet in our section. I pulled my sketchbook out and turned to an empty sheet.

"Hey, Rayne."

I turned around when I heard the familiar voice. My coworker Kyle walked over into our section. I faked a smile; the last thing I wanted was Kyle in my face. He was sweet, but also a bit creepy. We called him "Myron" behind his back because he sometimes reminded us of Diamond's stalker in the movie *The Players Club*. He was nice, but never could take a clue. He was a sad case; not ugly but very sloppy in the way he presented himself. His low self-esteem reeked through, but he would always try to impress the most beautiful girls in the call center by spoiling us with various treats. Even with his weirdness he was a nice guy overall but just needed some work.

"What's up, Kyle."

Kyle made it all the way to my chair. I noticed he was holding a newspaper rolled up. "I was reading and came across this." Kyle handed me the newspaper.

I opened it to see a large article with my picture along with a few others. My eyes widened. I stared at the photo I had taken over a month ago.

"Time is ticking away I see." Kyle smiled.

"What's that?"

I looked at Loyal who was attempting to read over my shoulder.

"Oh nobody told you?" Kyle smiled. "You are sitting next to our artist superstar."

"Whatever." I rolled my eyes as I kept reading the paper.

"Artist?" Loyal stared at me.

"Yeah." Kyle turned his attention to the new guy. "Rayne is an amazing artist. She's going to be featured in the Best of Memphis show at the Brooks in a month."

"Really now?" His eyes were burning a hole in the side of my face.

I turned my head only to meet his stare right on. He nodded his head obviously impressed by all the boasting Kyle was doing. I didn't know why I suddenly started feeling uneasy. I focused back on my article. I listened as Kyle continued to sing my praises like he was a proud father or husband. I just shook my head, hoping he would stop at some point. Thank goodness breaks were only fifteen minutes. Finally Kyle headed back to the other side of the office to his cubicle.

"So that's what you are always doing in that book."

I looked up to catch eye contact with Loyal again. His eyes were fixated on me. The uneasy feeling was settling back over me. "Yeah, but I just sketch a bit while at work." I stared back at my paper.

"That is really amazing. So you are like a real-life Picasso."

"I wouldn't go that far." I picked up my pencil trying not to look back at him.

"So what is your style?"

Why was he asking so many questions? I had never wanted my phone to ring so badly in my life. Why did they have to sit him next to me? He's way too talkative for my liking. Not to mention I, for some reason, didn't think I could lie to him.

I didn't know why but I picked my sketchpad up and handed it over to him. I rarely showed people my sketchpad. I had a thing about people seeing unfinished work.

Loyal began to turn through my pages. I watched as he studied my sketches like he was at an actual gallery. I couldn't help but notice his jaw line. His face was chiseled with amazing lines. I could easily recreate his image in clay. His hands caught my eye. I cringed at the sight.

"You are in total need of this." I handed him my jar of body butter.

Loyal looked down at his hands. "Yeah, you are right. I washed my hands in the bathroom and didn't have lotion."

I put a dab of my cream on my finger and wiped it into his hand. The inside of his hands were hard. "Eww what is up with your hands, dude? Do you never use lotion?"

Loyal laughed. "It's from working out. I gotta get some new gloves."

"So you work out a lot?" I looked down at my stomach. I felt a wave of insecurity take over my body. I pulled down on my shirt trying to camouflage my belly as much as I could.

"Every day."

"I need to be doing the same thing," I shyly admitted to him.

"Well, if you ever want to, we can. Just let me know."

"Loyal."

We both turned around when a woman's voice called his name. A girl I had never seen was walking up holding a bag in her hand. She wasn't anything special to look at, dark skinned, so skinny I knew I could probably see her ribs if she took off the dress she was wearing. She was a girly girl with a face full of makeup and heels that looked more like a weapon than shoes.

Loyal handed me my sketchpad and I quickly turned back to my desk. I began to sketch in my book again while one ear focused on their conversation.

"I thought you might want this." The girl handed the bag to Loyal. He looked in it.

"Oh, sure, thanks." He opened the Rubbermaid container. I could smell the chicken. It actually smelled pretty good.

"I made too much last night and I know you like to eat so I figured I'd share." I could see the girl look at me out of my periphery. "How you liking it over here?"

"It's cool, it's cool. Well yeah, thanks for the food. I'll bring the container back to you."

"You can keep it." She smiled. "I cook so much I have a bunch of them."

The girl finally walked away. I watched as Loyal inspected the chicken and then frowned. He took the chicken out of the container, threw the chicken in the bag, and put the bag in the trash. He looked up at me as I just stared.

"What?"

"That is so wrong." I laughed. "How you gon' act all happy to get it then throw it away?"

"I don't eat everyone's cooking." Loyal pulled a familiar green box out of the bag.

The fat girl in me took over instantly as I jumped up out of my seat. Loyal's phone rang before I could ask him for some of his Thin Mints Girl Scout Cookies.

I stood behind his chair while he listened to the customer on the phone. I figured I would sweet talk him the same way I sweet talked my gay male best friend. I put my hands on each of his shoulders and began to massage them slowly. Loyal's head dropped. I heard a slight quiver in his voice as he struggled to gain his composure on the phone. Not expecting that response I sat back down to let him finish his call.

Loyal's chair turned to me the second he said good-bye. "What in the hell?" His voice seemed to go an octave higher.

"I was just trying to get you to give me some cookies." I smiled.

Loyal looked at the box of cookies on his desk. He picked them up and threw them on my desk. "Woman, you can have the cookies. Hell you can have anything if you just do that again. Oh my goodness, I wasn't expecting that at all."

I blushed. "It was just a little massage."

"No, wasn't nothing little about that. You almost made me lose my entire cool on the phone. Damn, girl, what do you not do?"

I opened the box of cookies and bit into one of the tasty morsels. I glanced down at my stomach. "Exercise." I frowned. "I guess these cookies are the last thing I need."

"No, I don't think those are diet Girl Scout Cookies." We both laughed.

Loyal's eyes were fixated on me. The few hairs on my arm stood on edge. It had been a long time but I had this strange feeling that he was actually flirting with me.

"So when do I get to see some of the actual art?"

Loyal was too close for comfort. I could smell his cologne. He smelled really good. I was becoming suspicious. Why was he sitting so close to me and acting the way he was? He knew I was gay. I know he heard the discussion the other day that Camille brought up about trying to hook me up with a girl she knew. He was listening just like everyone else in my area as I told her that I would never date anyone she tried to hook me up with.

"Why are you so interested in my work?"

There was brief pause. Loyal's eyes locked on me. I couldn't help but look at him in his eyes. I tried to look away but something was compelling me not to move.

"Because, Rayne, I find you very intriguing."

He didn't take his eyes off of me. I wanted to look away but the force had me spellbound. The sound of his phone ringing finally broke the connection. I quickly turned back to my desk. I didn't know what just happened but I didn't want it to happen again.

A burst of callers kept us busy for the rest of the night. It seemed like whenever I got a free minute he was on a call. Finally it was time to call it a night. I packed up all of my things while he turned in our paperwork for the day.

"So what are you getting into tonight?" Loyal asked me as he picked up his keys and fedora hat.

"Work as usual." I zipped my book bag and placed it over my shoulder.

"Cool, cool. Have a good night, Ms. Rayne." Loyal winked his right eye at me as he walked away from our bay. I got this sudden urge to follow him but I resisted. I grabbed the last of my items and headed out the door.

I sighed as soon as I got out of the door. I had forgotten to move my car from the end of the parking lot. It was darker than usual as two of the streetlamps were obviously out near my car. I tried to wait a moment in case security drove around but they seemed to be nowhere to be found. I knew I was just going to have to make the long trek.

"Don't tell me that's your car all the way down there."

To my right I saw the window of Loyal's black Camry roll down. I didn't know why his car surprised me. I had pictured him in something a lot sportier or a large SUV.

"Yeah, I don't know what I was thinking." I walked down the three steps.

"I'll give you a ride down. Come on."

I could feel my stomach knotting up but I couldn't for the life of me figure out why. I opened the passenger door and got in. His car looked like it had just left the showroom floor. There wasn't a single piece of paper out of place. My car was the total opposite; in fact if anyone attempted to sit in the passenger side they would have to move a pile of art supplies first.

"You know you could move your car down at lunchtime. That's what normal people do." Loyal smiled.

"I know. I was sketching and time got away from me." I suddenly noticed we weren't headed toward my car.

"I'm taking the scenic route." He smiled again. I couldn't argue with him considering I was now in his car. To my surprise he drove all the way around our long building in silence. I didn't know why my palms were tensing up. I rubbed my hands together.

"Are you cold?" Loyal asked when he saw what I was doing.

"No, my hand was tensing up."

"Carpal tunnel?"

"No, anxiety from this possible kidnapping."

Loyal laughed. He turned the corner and I could see my car in the distance. "I'm not kidnapping you. Just wanted to occupy a little more of your time."

"Why?" I turned my body toward him. "Loyal, in the last few weeks I've seen I know at least four different girls come to your desk. So why are you attempting to take my time?"

"I already told you I find you intriguing."

"Yeah, okay, I'm intriguing, and I'm also very gay. You know this right?"

"I'm sorry, was me finding you intriguing the same thing as me trying to hook up with you?" Loyal's smile faded to a more serious look.

"Well, I've never known a guy try to take a scenic route with a girl he wasn't trying to get with."

"I'm not trying to get with you, Rayne. I just think you are cool as shit and I'd really love to see some of your art sometime."

He pulled his car into the spot next to mine. I stared at the side of his face again. Loyal turned his face toward me. I knew why women were so drawn to him; he was beautiful.

"Thanks for the ride. Sorry about all the other."

"It's cool, Rayne. You get home safely all right? See you Monday."

I got out of his car and closed the door. I realized I didn't have my keys in my hand. I pulled my book bag off and began to rummage through it for my keys.

"Damn, girl, don't tell me you don't have your keys."

I felt my keys and pulled them out of my bag. I dangled them in the air and smiled. I pressed my keyless entry as Loyal started to roll his window back up. This unsettling feeling came over my body. I wasn't ready for him to leave me.

"Loyal!"

Loyal stopped his car from backing up. He pulled back up and rolled his window all the way back down.

"Did you really want to see my work?"

Chapter 4

I couldn't believe this man was in my place. I stood back against my door as Loyal walked around my art space. I watched him study my projects that I had finished in my gallery living room in my house. I felt uneasy. The only people who ever came in my apartment were close friends and family. Now I had someone who was practically a stranger staring at my work.

"I love this one." Loyal pointed to a painting on my wall.

I smiled. "That's one of my favorites too. What do you see in it?" I loved asking people that question. The abstract art could mean anything to anyone but it was fun watching people attempt to see what I was seeing when I created it. I noticed that Loyal wasn't smiling.

"I don't see anyone or any specific thing. I just see . . . sadness."

My eyes widened as Loyal broke my piece down like he was a professional.

"The blue swirls start to crack bleeding in red. I think that's a broken heart. And the black coming in at the end, to me that's just emptiness. There is no more heart at all, just darkness."

I was speechless. This man read my painting to the tee.

"Who was it?"

"Who was what?" I turned my head toward him. Loyal was staring at me with his same intense glare.

"Who broke your heart?"

I took a step back. No one had read my painting perfectly before or could tell that it was completely about me.

"I want to show you something." I pulled the door to my working space open. I turned the light on and watched as Loyal's eyes popped as he walked into my studio. I could tell he was surprised I was allowing him to see this space.

"You sculpt, too." Loyal walked straight toward the torso and hands I had been working on.

"Yeah, it's something I'm working on. I don't really know where it came from. I just got this image in my head and felt like I needed to sculpt it."

"That is so damn bad ass." Loyal stared at the clay.

I walked closer to him. "Thank you. I don't really know what I'm going to do with it. I can't seem to get past this part of it."

"You blocked or something?" Loyal looked at me.

"It came in a dream and I haven't had the dream again. So yeah, I guess you can call it blocked. Plus it's not anything like the other stuff I'm working for the show so I probably shouldn't be focused on it anyway."

I walked over to the other side of the room and pulled a white sheet off of a canvas I had been working on.

"Can I say something to you without you getting offended?" Loyal's voice echoed through the room. I could hear his footsteps coming toward me.

"What's up?" I didn't know why I couldn't bring myself to turn away from the painting. I stared at it even as he came closer and closer. Loyal was standing right behind me, so close I could almost feel him.

"You are blocked because you need some sex."

"What?" I still couldn't turn to him. I felt him take another step closer. He put his index finger on the nape of my neck causing my body to shiver.

"See. That reaction in itself lets me know you are in definite need of some really good sex."

I forced myself to turn around. Our eyes met, our bodies so close I could feel the heat coming from him. I pushed him back. "Oh, so that's what this about? You wanted to come here so you could try to seduce the gay girl?"

"No. I didn't say you needed sex from me. I said you just need sex in general. I don't know why you feel like I'm trying to fuck you, Rayne."

"Because of shit like that whole touching my neck thing. Come on, Loyal, you are not stupid. Every girl gets heated when a person touches them there. The nape of the neck is worse than a forehead kiss."

Loyal nodded his head. The right side of his mouth curled up into a grin. "Rayne, sweetie, I'm not trying to fuck you." Loyal walked back over to the painting. "I think you are very talented but honestly you are not my type."

The words felt like a punch in my gut. I knew deep down that someone as gorgeous as Loyal would never be interested in the big girl who sat next to him, no matter how talented I might be. I didn't know if my face showed my feelings but Loyal immediately started shaking his head.

"I know you think that it's probably because of your size but it's not. You are not my type because you are gay and you work with me. I don't need those types of problems."

"What does that mean?"

Loyal sat down on my stool. He put his head down to think for a moment before raising it back to look at me. "You said yourself, you've seen like at least four girls at my desk. Well take that number and multiply it by at least seven and you will have the amount of women who try to get at me on a daily basis. The ones who I have messed off with are still trying to get it again. When was the last time you were with a man?"

"Fourteen years."

"Yeah, no." Loyal shook his head. "Hell no, I might as well be fucking a virgin. I don't want those problems."

"So you think if I let you fuck me I would be all dickmatized or something?"

"Rayne, I don't think. I know."

I couldn't help but laugh. I couldn't believe the audacity of this guy to sit in my house and speak so cocky about himself. I started thinking about the two guys I had actually had sex with in my life. Both of them boasted about their sexual ability but I was left highly unsatisfied both times. I didn't even let my women strap or penetrate me because the thought of vaginal sex was appalling to me.

"Okay, Loyal, whatever you say." I picked up the sheet and placed it back over my painting. I suddenly had an attitude.

"What is wrong with you?" Loyal's ability to pick up on everything about me was starting to piss me off.

"Because honestly I think you are full of shit. I think you came over here with intentions of seeing how hot and bothered you could make the lesbian just to see if you could. But I also think you never had any intention of trying me because like most you aren't attracted to big girls. That whole spiel you gave was some bullshit and you know it."

"Rayne, this has nothing to do with your body."

"That's what they all say." I could almost envision my last girlfriend standing in the same place he was standing feeding me all the similar garbage as to why we just weren't going to work out. In the end she left me for a size-six girl with long weave and fake eyelashes.

"Take off your clothes."

I knew I didn't hear him right. I turned around to see Loyal staring at me with an even deeper intensity.

"Excuse me?" I felt my hands tensing up again.

"I said take off your clothes, Rayne."

"What?"

Loyal stood up. He started to walk toward me. I looked to my right and left. I had nowhere to run to.

"You want real, so I'm going to give you real. Your work is amazing, but it also is like looking directly into your soul." Loyal pointed at the other sculptures in the room. "Look at your work. The hands are all very similar until you get to this new one."

I felt my heart starting to race. Loyal walked up until our bodies were almost touching.

"That one, you weren't dreaming of a girl. You were dreaming of a man."

"No."

"Yes." Loyal nodded his head. "You know I am right. The body, the hands, it's you and it's a man's hands on you. Rayne, you may not be straight. But your body is yearning for something stronger than you are used to."

Loyal put his hands on my sides. I felt a wave of emotion come over me. He held on to my sides tight, gripping my thickness with his strong hands. Loyal pulled me into him. I couldn't resist. I didn't want to.

"See? Your mind might not know what you want. But your body sure does. Now let me see you."

I couldn't respond. I didn't know what was happening. This beautiful man was in my personal space, holding on to me like I belonged to him. My brain was telling me to stop, but my body was telling me to give him whatever he wanted.

Loyal tried to pull my shirt over my head but I pulled away. I took a few steps back.

"What are you doing?" he questioned.

"I don't let anyone see me naked."

"Wait what?" Loyal looked confused.

"I don't get naked."

"When you are having sex you don't get naked?" He cocked his head to the side.

"No. I always have on a shirt."

"What type of punk bitches are you messing with?" Loyal rushed up on me. He pulled me close again. "I want to see you." He pulled at my shirt again.

I pulled away again. "I said I don't get naked."

"Rayne."

A deep silence came over the room as we stared at each other. Loyal walked up to me again. He didn't grab me this time. He placed his hands on my sides again. I felt an unusual sensation come over me. I felt extremely comfortable. Loyal slowly pulled my shirt over my head. I allowed the shirt to come off. I stood there with just my jeans and bra. I tried to put my hands in front of my stomach to camouflage my rolls.

Loyal sat down on the stool in front of me. He pulled my hands down. I watched as he stared at my body. He began to explore my upper body with his hands. His hands felt different, mainly from the hardness from working out with no gloves. His hands rested on my sides. Loyal pulled me into him again. His mouth met my right side. He kissed my side before he started to suck in the same place. I felt my knees trying to give way. I held on to his broad shoulders with my hands until he pulled away.

"Just so you know, your size has absolutely nothing to do with anything. I don't give a fuck about your size. Only bitch-ass people give a damn about how a person looks and they don't deserve you to begin with."

Loyal stood up with my shirt in his hand. He put it back over my head as I put my arms back into the sleeves. I didn't know what was happening. Why was he dressing me? I knew it had been awhile but I thought more clothes were supposed to come off.

"You are an amazing girl, Rayne." Loyal pulled me close hugging me.

I put my arms around him, accepting his strong embrace. I couldn't remember the last time I felt so safe in a person's arms. He kissed me on my forehead just to further fuck with me. Loyal took me by my hand and led me out of the room and to my front door.

I was dumfounded. I knew I had to be having an out-of-body experience. We couldn't really be walking to the front door like he was about to leave. But another piece of me was just completely confused by the whole thing. Why did I want this man to stay?

"Thank you for letting me see all of this. I really do feel special right now."

Loyal was back in his usual professional mode. I wanted to shake the shit out of him. Not only did he just see my body, and kiss me like I had never been kissed before, but now he wanted to leave like it never happened.

"Umm, okay." I didn't know what else to say. I wasn't going to beg him to stay, even in this heated state; I wasn't the type of girl to beg anyone for anything. And in my brain I knew it was a good thing that he left. I didn't know what any of this night meant. I needed time to process.

I watched him walk out the door. I closed my door behind him. I couldn't move. I stood against the door trying to replay the night in my head. This wasn't making sense in my head. I just let a man see me half naked and I let him kiss me in a place most had never seen before. But what was more perplexing to me was that he didn't try anything more with me. This wasn't the way I remembered men to be. I finally forced myself to walk back to my studio.

In just a few minutes my world was turned upside down. I couldn't come to terms with the feelings I was having. I was nervous because a man had just left my house, yet I was anxious because I wanted him to stay. I was also mad at myself that I let him touch me, but angrier that he left me hot and bothered. Was I actually interested in a guy? Still the thought of a penis anywhere near me made my stomach turn, but his hands on me felt so comfortable, and familiar.

I sat down in front of the sculpture. I picked up my scalpel and carved out small markings. I looked at it to see a perfect set of bite marks on the right side. I couldn't help but smile as I touched my own skin. I didn't think I ever felt the feeling he had given me with just that simple touch. Out of all the emotions going through me one stood out more than any. I was curious.

Chapter 5

Monday came quicker than I expected. I got a good amount of work done but also was able to get some really good sleep in. I found myself not wanting to wake up most times. My dreams were back. Now I had a face to go with the hands. I could picture Loyal's eyes, lips, and the amazing arms he had. I couldn't believe I was lusting over a man.

It didn't hit me until I saw his car parked in the lot. I was about to be face to face with the guy who had opened my personal Pandora's box. I wasn't ready to see him. I pulled a brush out of my car and brushed my hair back before putting a headband on to hide my edges. I grabbed a small compact of eye shadow and put a little pink on to match my pink shirt. I put some lip gloss on before realizing I only had a few minutes to get into work.

"Oh shhh now!"

I stopped in my tracks at the sound of Camille's loud voice. I turned to see her and another coworker, Sabrina, walking toward me. Both were smiling and pointing at me.

"Bitch, who you dressing up for?" Camille ran her fingers through my hair.

"You look so pretty, Rayne." Sabrina always gushed whenever I put on makeup.

"Girl, please, where is your eyeliner and mascara?" Camille frowned. "You are an artist; you of all people should be able to paint your damn face."

I could see Loyal standing by our desks. He was laughing with Janice and Rosalyn. My heart skipped a beat. I tried to hold my smile in. I didn't want to let anyone know what or who I was smiling at.

"Y'all about to make me late for work." I walked away as quickly as I could. I could feel Camille following me. Everyone in my section was laughing at something.

"What's so funny?" I asked as I set my bag down on my desk.

"We are laughing at Romeo over here." Janice continued to chuckle. "He comes in and finds this Edible Arrangement on his desk but claims he doesn't know where it came from."

"I don't." Loyal's and my eyes met.

"You got it like that, Loyal?" Camille joined in. "Pretty-ass nigga got secret admirers and shit. Hell why isn't it open? Can a girl get a strawberry?"

Loyal let the women have their way with the Edible Arrangement. I watched them make fun of him and his admirers.

"As long as they bring food I'm totally cool with them coming over here." Janice took a bite of a pineapple sun.

"Oh so as long as you guys get to eat it's okay. But the second they come empty-handed . . ."

"It's a wrap." Janice and Loyal both laughed.

"Would you like some?" Loyal said to me as I got my computer turned on. I shook my head no.

I didn't know how I was feeling in that moment. I wasn't dumb and I had seen the women before. Could this really just be a secret admirer or was it something more? I felt my eyes trying to turn green but I wouldn't let them. This wasn't my man; he wasn't even someone I was dating. At that point Loyal was just a coworker who happened to see me semi-nude.

The rest of the day was going rather smoothly. Our coworkers were all off leaving us for the night haul. I ended a phone call with a customer who just wanted to complain about everything. I listened to the man complain about getting a renewal notice in the mail because we shouldn't be sending mail to save the planet. I finally got off the phone and took a deep sigh.

"Pineapple?"

I turned to see Loyal holding the last of the arrangement in his hand. "Why not." I pulled a pineapple off of the stick. I bit into the juicy fruit causing some of the juice to run down the side of my mouth. Loyal smiled and shook his head.

"Let me get that." With his thumb Loyal caught the juice flowing down the side of my face. He looked at me before placing his thumb in his mouth. "Tastes good."

I felt my body trying to betray me. I shifted in my seat as my panties moistened. "You are an ass." I turned back to my computer screen.

"Why am I an ass?" Loyal questioned.

"You know exactly why."

"Loyal."

We both turned when the same face from the other night was walking back toward us. I shook my head as I turned back to my computer screen. I listened as she asked him how he liked the food. I noticed how easily he lied to her. She then mentioned something about an invitation being open. He told her he would let her know. I wanted to scream. Out of all the men for me to have this weird crush on I would pick the one every girl in the call center was trying to get.

"So back to this whole ass thing." Loyal didn't skip a breath coming right back to me when she walked away.

"Don't you have an invitation to accept or something?" I picked up one of my pencils.

Loyal smiled. "Someone was listening way too hard. This is why I said what I said Friday night."

The comment made me do a quick turn in my chair. "First off, I couldn't help but hear. Good Lord, could you please give her some water 'cause she's thirsty as hell." Loyal laughed.

"Second, you don't know me. There hasn't been a man or woman the whole time I have dated who made me fall for them because of their sex. The reason for that is because I am not a sexual person. I honestly couldn't care less about sex."

"Is that right?" Loyal just smiled.

"It's right. I don't even like sex usually. I just do it to please the other person." I paused. I couldn't believe I said that out loud.

Loyal's smile faded as well. "That's not good, babe."

"Well, it's the truth. Sex is dumb and I don't understand the purpose of it. And yes, you can go right ahead and say that it must be the people I'm sleeping with just like everyone else says but it's not. I just don't like it."

"I am truly, truly sorry to hear that." Loyal put his hand on my knee. "Because the person you are with should make it their mission to make sure you love every moment of it."

I felt my panties moistening again. I looked into Loyal's beautiful eyes. I could tell he truly meant every word.

The night ended. We turned our paperwork in and went our separate ways. I noticed that Loyal always walked through the call center before heading out the door. I knew he was probably making his rounds, saying good night to all the women who he messed with.

The ride home seemed quicker than usual especially since I made a quick stop at the liquor store before going home. I popped open the bottle of Riesling and poured it into one of my larger wine glasses. Work was calling me. I knew I needed to get at least an hour in before calling it a night. My mind was restless thinking about the man who sat next to me at work. Why couldn't I stop thinking about him?

My doorbell rang causing me to leave my daydream state. I wasn't expecting anyone and it was much too late for any deliveries. Peeping through the peephole my heart dropped. There stood Loyal.

"You know I can hear you right?" He laughed.

I lowered my head and sighed; he busted me. With full pouty lip poked out I proceeded to open the door slightly. "What makes you think you can just show up at my crib?"

Loyal took a step back. His look let me know he knew he was coming in at some point. "I was in the area, I called, you didn't answer so I decided to take a chance. Got someone else over or something?"

"So that just gives you the right just to show up?" I held my ground, holding the door close to me.

The right side of Loyal's mouth curled up. He took a step closer to the door. "Okay, so are we going to continue this witty banter or are you going to let me in?"

For a moment I considered not letting him in. The last thing I wanted was some dude thinking he had the right to show up at my house unexpected. I didn't even let women I dated do that. Then I looked at his cute smile. Slowly the door opened and he walked in.

There we stood in the hallway again. My body was starting to betray me again with the anticipation of things that could happen. The sexual beast was having a full-fledged fight with the lesbian hard worker in me. This man was trouble and I knew it, but I couldn't seem to conjure the words to tell him to leave.

"What are you drinking?" Loyal took the glass from my hand and took a sip of my wine. He didn't take his eyes off of me. Was he trying me to see what I would do? Was the showing up and drinking out of my glass some type of test to see what type of woman I was?

"Why ask if you gon' just drink from my glass?" I grabbed my glass back and walked to my kitchen, his footsteps following me. I pulled another glass out and poured Loyal a glass of wine. My eyes followed him as the glass hit his thick lips.

"What are you doing in my area?" I questioned as I took another sip.

"I don't know really. I should be home but somehow I ended up all the way out here in Midtown. I was wondering if you could tell me the reason why?" Loyal's eyes locked on me.

My leg twitched. "Okay, so how about we keep it real then? What are you trying to accomplish here, Loyal? Is it 'turn out a lesbian' week for you or something?"

Loyal's laugh echoed through my kitchen and into the hallway. He walked closer putting his arm on my shoulder. "Rayne, can't I just want to be your friend and get to know you better? Why does there have to be an ulterior motive? We work together don't we? I already told you I'm not going to sleep with you."

"You aren't going to sleep with me but you can kiss my half-naked ass and shit. Get the fuck outta here with that." I pushed his arm off of me.

Loyal finished the glass of wine in one gulp. He put the glass down on my countertop. My arms were folded as I stared at him waiting to hear what he would come up with next.

"Rayne." Loyal smiled. "I told you already what the business is but that isn't good enough for you. So why don't you tell me what you want from me or what you want me to say?"

The question was harder than I thought. I didn't know what I wanted from him. One side of me wanted him to hold me like he did the other night, while another side wanted him to leave before things became complicated for real. This man had already seen more than any man. Why was I so comfortable with him?

"You got an answer because I would really like to know why the lesbian seems to be so concerned with why I won't try to bang her."

"Because . . ."

"Because what?" It was obvious he wasn't going to change the subject.

"I don't know." I threw my hands up in defeat.

Silence filled the room.

We didn't speak as Loyal took me by my hands and guided me into my living room. He motioned for me to sit next to him on the couch. He put his hands on my knees and stared deep into my eyes. "Rayne, talk to me. What's going on in that brilliant head of yours?"

He seemed so sincere I felt like I could tell him anything. "Loyal, I don't know what is happening to me. All I do know is that I haven't been touched or held the way you did the other day in . . . I honestly can't say when the last time was. I liked it. I don't know why, but I really liked it."

"So are you saying you want more than that?" He kept his eyes on me.

"I don't know what I want. I just know I liked that."

Loyal took his eyes off of me only to glance down for a quick second before focusing his attention back to me. He rubbed his hands on my knee. It was very endearing.

"Could it be that because you have been denying yourself pleasure for so long that now your body is craving it from anyone or anywhere?"

I shook my head. "I thought about that, but I see hundreds of people every day. Hell I get hit on all the time but I haven't been attracted to anyone outside of you." Loyal's devilish grin appeared. "So you admit you are attracted to me?" He winked.

I playfully hit him on his shoulder. "You already knew that, which is why you keep teasing me and shit."

We both laughed. The laugher was short as I quickly noticed the intense, serious look that appeared on his face.

"Rayne, you want me to keep it real with you. I will do that now. I think you are an amazing woman, and you are cool as shit. To me, that is sexier than any size six out there. I would like nothing more than to show you what real pleasure you have been missing out on for so long, but I just can't."

"Why?" I couldn't believe I asked the question. I found myself wanting to know why he was denying me what he claimed to want and what I was starting to believe I wanted just as bad.

"Rayne we have already gone over this."

"Well refresh my memory," I folded my arms.

"Well one, we work together and sit next to each other. You already know the business; yes, I fuck off with other woman up there and that isn't going to change. I don't give a fuck about those bitches; most I fuck and never talk to again. With you I wouldn't want to do that because I actually want to develop a friendship with you. Plus on top of all of that you haven't been with a man in so fucking long, it would be like I'm with a virgin and that brings a whole different group of issues. I can fuck you; I can make you feel like you have never felt before. But I will never be a boyfriend or anything like a boyfriend. And no matter what your mouth says I know in the end you aren't going to be satisfied with that."

The words stuck in my brain. I figured he messed with other girls but since no one had ever made an actual claim to him I figured they were all just groupies. The second half then hit me. He didn't want to sleep with me because he thought I would catch feelings. Crazy enough, denying me only made me want him even more.

"Loyal . . ." I said as I stood up. I began to pace the floor. I wanted to make sure the right words came out. I finished off the last of my wine. My body was aching for some affection and it was calling Loyal's name. In that moment nothing else mattered. I didn't care that I was a lesbian or that we worked together. I could feel the aggressive side of me coming out. He had laid a challenge without even knowing it.

"I get everything you are saying and yes, it all makes perfect sense. However, there are a few things you are saying that I need to correct. Like I said earlier I am not driven by sex. Sex is not something that will ever or has ever made me fall for a person. If I fell for you it would be you as a person not what you do to my body. Second, I don't want to be your girlfriend. I have a career I am trying to launch and nothing is more important than that. The most I could possibly be is a fluffer."

"A fluffer?" Loyal questioned.

"Yes. You know how in porn there are the girls who get the guys ready for the main scenes? Well, the most you would be able to do is come by, knock me off something, then go your merry way."

I never heard him laugh so hard before. I watched as he cracked up over my fluffer statement. It took him a minute to gain his composure after the laugh.

"Rayne, I hear what you are saying but you gotta understand how many times I have heard that."

"So you are judging me off other women?" I crossed my arms.

"I am just saying I am trying to protect you from yourself here."

I wasn't sure where the aggressive side was coming from. I sat back down next to Loyal. Curiosity was about to kill my cat and I didn't care. "Maybe I don't want or need to be protected."

I put my hands on his True Religion jeans. I unbuttoned the top button and pulled the zipper down. Loyal shook his head, but didn't resist what I was doing. I smiled. Just like I thought everything about him was polished; even his briefs were Ralph Lauren. My hand slid down the inside of his pants. I was shocked at the thickness I felt. I wasn't an expert but I knew that had to be pretty big.

"Rayne."

I ignored him calling my name. I pulled his erect penis out of the slit in his briefs. My eyes bulged as I saw it for the first time. It was bigger than even I had imagined. There was no way I thought that thing was ever going to fit inside of me.

"Scared yet?" Loyal smiled.

"A little bit," I replied.

"Don't be. Come here."

Loyal pulled me closer to him. I knew what was coming next. His hand touched the back of my head. I pulled back quickly.

"I don't know what I am doing."

"Just try," Loyal said as he pulled my head closer.

It was now or never. I tried to remember the last time I ever gave head. It was something I used to do just to get out of having sex with my boyfriends. I would always prefer giving head over penetration. I closed my eyes and opened my mouth.

To my surprise his penis didn't have a smell or bad taste. There wasn't any unwanted hair as his manhood was just as manicured as the rest of him.

I licked the tip, tasting a bit of pre-cum coming out of the tip. My lips wrapped around his shaft. I let the tip of my tongue graze his protruding vein as I sucked his dick. I heard him moan my name. I stopped and looked up at him. He opened his eyes.

"Why did you stop?" he whispered.

"I didn't know if I was doing it right." I tried to study his face to see if I was actually pleasing him.

"If you weren't, I would tell you," Loyal whispered.

This pleased me. I suddenly wanted to please him more. I got on my knees in front of him. I held on to his shaft with my left hand while my mouth worked up and down with the flow of my hand movements. With every moan I only wanted to please him more. I wasn't surprised. The sounds of a woman moaning always made me want to please them more. I was just shocked it was working on a man as well.

I wondered how deep I could go. I pushed his dick deep inside my mouth until I couldn't take anymore. I could feel myself about to gag. I came back up for air before trying again. He let out a louder moan as his hand tried to push my head deeper again. I pushed up for air without letting go of his hard erection.

He was lasting longer than any guy I'd known in my high school years. I jacked him off while sucking his thick penis but there were no signs of him cuming anytime soon. My panties were soaking wet. I wanted more. I wanted to feel his hands on me. I pulled back and looked at him. His eyes were bright with astonishment.

"Damn, girl. Are you sure you are gay?" Loyal shook his head as I sat back on the couch. "Fuck, girl, that was amazing."

"Quit playing." I shrugged my shoulders. I didn't need him trying to gas my head up.

"I am not."

The look on his face made me believe he was telling the truth.

Out of nowhere Loyal pushed me back on the couch. He pulled my shirt over my head and pulled my bra up exposing both of my breasts. His big hands held on to my DDDs with force as his mouth became very familiar with my right nipple. I bit my lip. It was much more aggressive than with any stud I had ever dated. His hands could easily hold on to my large breast, and his mouth commanded them with vengeance.

I suddenly wanted even more. I wanted to know what his mouth would feel like in other areas. I needed head and I needed it bad. I mimicked him from earlier, putting my hand on his head and pushing him down to my area. He moved my hands from off his head and stared at me. He grabbed each of my legs and pulled me into his torso. Loyal buried his head in my panties, licking the wetness off of the cotton boy shorts. He pushed the small piece of fabric out of the way with his nose as his tongue entered my walls.

My mouth dropped as Loyal began to lick me with an aggression I definitely wasn't used to. It felt a bit strange. I could feel the small hairs pricking me from his goatee. The softness I was used to was gone; there was nothing soft about the way he licked me. I felt my stomach starting to knot up. My legs began to tremble. If his tongue skills were any indication of the rest of his sexual prowess I knew now why women would fall for him.

My right leg jerked with every nibble. My left leg quivered with each figure eight on my clit. He pressed his lips tight on my clit as he stuck his right index finger inside of me. My body was on high alert. I wanted to run so I began to scoot my butt back on the couch.

"No, you asked for it." Loyal came up for breath long enough to utter the statement before reclaiming my pussy as his personal property. He held on to my legs, locking me in so I couldn't move. My legs began to tense as my toes curled. I hit his massive arms but my hits were ignored. My mouth dropped as I flooded in his mouth.

"Damn, girl."

I couldn't move. Finally after a minute I opened my eyes to find him looking at me. I looked down to see my wetness all over his white tee. I covered my mouth in embarrassment.

"I'm so sorry." I wanted to stand up but my legs wouldn't let me.

"It's cool. You really did need that." Loyal stood up and pulled the white tee over his head. For the first time I got to admire his upper body completely naked. He was a vision. I could see each line where his muscles protruded. His stomach was chiseled, with a six pack most men only achieved with Photoshop.

"I actually have a shirt you can have."

My legs began to work again as Loyal helped me off the couch. He followed me to my bedroom where I pulled a white tee out of a bag that was still in the plastic wrapping.

"What do you just keep them around for times like this?" Loyal laughed.

"No, ass, I keep them for my work. I work in them."

Loyal put the tee over his head. I suddenly felt embarrassed by the way the shirt swallowed him.

"So when are you going to work out with me?" I sat on the edge of my bed.

"When you are really ready to work out." Loyal sat next to me. With his finger he turned my head around toward his face. He made eye contact and didn't take his eyes off of mine.

"Rayne, I will help you in whatever way you want. You want to get healthy that's cool, but do it for that reason and not because you just want to be skinny. Did it seem like I had any problem with your body earlier?"

I shook my head. He didn't skip a beat when going down on me, which was a change for me. I was used to people pausing, wondering if the big girl was going to suffocate them or smell bad. The oral sex no longer mattered to me. Loyal was pulling at my emotional strings with just being kind.

We walked to my hallway. I was starting to dread the entrance to my house. Loyal put his arms around me, pulling me close into him. "You promise not to change on me?"

"I promise."

With that he sealed the night with a deep, longing kiss. I didn't want the kiss to end, and I didn't want him to leave. I stood by the door for a few moments. I closed my eyes hoping he might surprise me and knock back on the door. After a few moments I finally gained all my composure back. I felt artistic. I headed straight into my studio and back to the sculpture.

I began to wet the bottom portion of the sculpture until it began to move. The clay began to form with my touch. I no longer wanted to stop at the torso, it needed to show more. I formed thighs, thick legs that weren't perfect by any means. I didn't smooth them; I let the clay form the tiny dimples in various portions of the legs. I formed a delicate vagina hump in the middle. I thought about making it more realistic but changed my mind.

My clock went off alerting me that once again time had gotten away from me and it was three in the morning. I stretched. My body ached from sitting on the stool for such a long period of time. A cool breeze hit my body, catching the tiny hairs on the back of my neck. A feeling came over me, causing my stomach to knot up. I grabbed my stomach and closed my eyes.

Loyal was grabbing my body like it belonged to him. His hands pulled my legs causing me not to move. I could feel his head in between my legs, his mouth devouring me like I was the last meal he would ever enjoy. His strong hands grabbed my breasts with his thick index finger rubbing my swollen nipples.

I inhaled and opened my eyes. It was all a dream. He wasn't there but I felt him as much in that moment as I did earlier that night. A very uneasy feeling was settling over me. I was a fish in shark territory and I couldn't help but think that I would be the one hurt in the end.

Chapter 6

Why were wedding shops so white? I sat in the fancy bridal shop while my best friend tried on what had to be the thousandth dress. The white couch made me nervous. Why people insisted on white couches I would never understand.

"All right this one isn't so bad." Bianca walked out in a mermaid-style dress with a tulle bottom. The top was covered in rhinestones, which I knew was right up her alley. She insisted on trying on dresses in all the major stores in Memphis and Atlanta just because she could. Bianca was rich and marrying a very wealthy up-and-coming surgeon. What he and her fabulous family didn't know was that we met at a gay club dancing on the floor where by the end of the night I had my fingers inside of her in a booth in the back of the club. We screwed around a few times after that before becoming really good friends.

"Bianca, seriously, you are about to make me kill you."

"You don't like it?"

Even the attendants rolled their eyes at her statement.

"Bitch, we have been in this store for almost two hours. You have tried on some of the exact same dresses you have tried on in other stores. I am not about to go through this with you."

Bianca curled her stringy blond hair around her finger. She turned to both sides to get a full look at the dress.

"I really did want to go ball gown," Bianca said as she bit her bottom lip.

"Kill me now." I fell back on the couch.

I pulled out my sketchpad and a pencil. I began to sketch a quick dress on the pad. The attendant assigned to us walked over, admiring my drawing. Bianca sat next to me as I designed her ball gown dress that was fit for the princess she thought she was.

"This is what I imagine for you, my friend. The bottom is big, ball gown, to give you that classic romance but with a halter neckline for your sexy side and because, well we know how you like to push those bad boys up." I smiled at Bianca who was grinning from ear to ear.

The attendant motioned for someone to come over but I continued to draw.

"The top should be covered in crystals because we both know you aren't wearing something that isn't."

"My friend knows me so well." Bianca playfully hit my shoulder.

We both looked up to see the assistant standing with the male manager and another woman who I figured was the seamstress by the pins stuck on her smock. I held the picture up. "Do you guys have anything that is similar?"

"Not similar. I want this."

I noticed how quickly Bianca went from playful to power bitch when she wanted something. That was one of the things I learned from being around her. When you have money the world is yours. In moments a team was together bringing fabric samples and similar dresses to the one I designed. My mind drifted off while Bianca pointed her fingers and had things her way. I couldn't help but wonder what Loyal was doing. I had taken the day off to be with Bianca, but the real reason was simple: I just wasn't ready to be around him.

"And where did you go just now?"

I looked up to see Bianca plop down on the couch right next to me. She laid her head on my shoulder.

"I don't know really."

"You are lying." Bianca smiled. "Who is she?"

I looked at my friend with her big smile and pretty blue eyes. She was who I could see Loyal messing with, not me. "What if I was to say it's not a she?"

Bianca's eyes popped open. Her smile turned into a perfect circle as her mouth dropped open. "What do you mean? It's not a man." Bianca sat up and turned her body toward me.

I knew I needed to tell someone. Bianca continued to point and shake her head as she hung on to every word I was telling her. I needed to tell someone about what I was doing before I completely lost my mind.

"This is bad isn't it?" I lowered my head. "Here I am on the brink of what might be my biggest break ever and I'm getting involved in some illicit affair."

"Wait what exactly makes it illicit?" Bianca's lip curled. "Nothing about what you are doing is illicit. Hell I'm actually proud of you."

"What do you mean?"

"Oh, sweetie, I don't know when you went from being the chick I met at the club to this recluse you are but it's about time you snap out of it." Bianca held her arms out for the seamstress.

"I am not a recluse. I just have my work—"

"Blah, blah, blah. You and your work. Did it ever occur to you that maybe getting some might actually help with your work? Why do you think most artists are freaks, alcoholics, or drug addicts? Sex is a liberating experience every time you have it. Am I not right?"

In unison the workers around us all agreed.

"Yeah, but think of some of the women we know. I'm not trying to end up all dickmatized wanting sex all day and not getting any work done."

"Now that"—Bianca pointed at me—"is entirely up to you. I'm not telling you to try to make this a real thing. Hell from what you say he wouldn't be main-guy material to begin with. However, he sounds like the perfect maintenance man. Wait . . . maybe this is a bad idea."

I gave Bianca an inquisitive look as she tried to change her mind.

"Rayne, can you mess with anyone and not catch feelings?"

"Get the fuck out of here, Bianca; of course I can."

"No, seriously, girl." Bianca sat back down. "Yeah, back in the day; but since Tee I don't know if you can."

I swallowed the knot in my throat at the mention of my ex. I knew exactly where Bianca was coming from. Tee was never supposed to be more than just a fling. I caught feelings and started wanting more. I gave her more without realizing I wasn't getting anything more in the process. In the end I was left with a broken heart and she moved on to the relationship she actually wanted.

"Trust me; I am never getting into another relationship like that again. In fact the second I notice I like a person more than they like me I'm leaving."

"Well in that case I say go for it. Let that man please you; who knows, you might actually like it."

After the long day I decided to go back home and relax. I didn't want to work on anything. I just wanted to get some much-needed R&R. I finally caught up on a few television shows I had missed in the last few weeks and checked my cluttered mail inbox. I caught myself checking the time. Loyal would be getting off soon and I couldn't help but wonder if he would contact me.

I decided I would be prepared for anything. I double-checked all important areas for any unwanted hair.

Next I took a long shower and opted for my coconut body wash and matching lotion. Once I smelled like piña colada I sprayed my body with the matching body splash just to add one more layer of yummyness.

Loyal was finally off work. I wondered would he actually call or just pull another pop-up like he did the previous night. I put on my kimono robe, tying it so that it hung off my shoulder a little bit. I poured a glass of wine and sat on my couch waiting for something to happen. After an hour passed I started to get nervous.

I decided to take a chance. I picked up my phone and called him, but after two rings I was sent to voicemail. I couldn't believe he just sent me to voicemail. I realized how foolish I was. I was doing the thing I said I wasn't going to do. I amped myself up for a date that was never discussed let alone confirmed. Feeling like a complete idiot I retreated to my room.

My phone woke me up. I grabbed the phone noticing the time on my alarm clock said 1:39 a.m. I looked down to see Loyal's picture flashing across the screen. I sat up in the bed, cleared my throat and answered using my sexy half-asleep voice.

"Are you dead?"

"What do you mean?"

Loyal's words were slurred.

"Why are you calling me at almost two in the morning, Loyal?"

There was a pause. I could tell Loyal was in a car from the background noise.

"My bad, I figured you were still up working on art."

"Are you drunk?" I frowned.

"Why you say that?"

"You are slurring like hell, Loyal. Where are you?"

There was another long pause. "Outside your crib."

My heart began to race. I jumped out of the bed and put my kimono robe back on. I could hear him calling my name as I looked myself over in the mirror.

"Then bring your drunk ass in," I muttered as I pulled the satin bonnet off my head.

I'd never been so anxious for something in my life. I sprayed myself again with the coconut body splash and put a little lotion on my arms, breasts, and neck. Feeling like I had overdone it, I stood in my bathroom fanning my body for the smell to die down a bit. I heard a faint knock on my door. I took a deep breath to gain my composure and walked to the door.

I opened the door and Loyal stumbled in past me walking in like it was his house. He leaned against the wall in the hallway. I closed the door and walked past him. He grabbed me and pulled me close causing goose bumps to cover my body.

Loyal placed his head on my shoulder. The tip of his nose grazed my ear. I could feel his breath on the side of my neck. "You smell good," he slurred.

"You're drunk."

"A little bit." Loyal took my hand. He walked down my hallway but passed the door for the living area and headed toward the bedroom.

"Where are you going?" I tried to hide my anticipation as he walked into my bedroom.

Loyal pulled his jacket off and hung it on my door. I watched as he pulled his pants and button-down off and laid them on a chair in my room. I hadn't seen him that naked before. His Ralph Lauren boxer briefs made his manhood look even bigger than I knew it to be. Loyal crawled on my bed and patted his hand against the mattress for me to join him.

I sat on the edge of the bed. I didn't know if I was ready for what was about to happen after all. Oral was one thing but did I really want to be penetrated by a man?

"Where is your remote?" Loyal felt around the bed.

I handed Loyal the remote. This wasn't going the way I expected. Loyal flipped through the channels and questioned me on how much I was paying to have so many channels. He settled on reruns of *The Boondocks*.

My mind was racing. What was I supposed to do? Did he really come over just to sober up with me and watch television or was this going to turn into a night of some kind of passion soon?

"Rayne." Loyal's voice awakened the beast in me. I turned to him allowing just a little bit of my breasts to be exposed from my robe. "Do you have any juice or water?"

I couldn't get into my kitchen quick enough. My feet paced the cold floor. This man was really lying up in my bed without making a move on me. Once again he had completely surprised me. A piece of me wanted to make a big deal but then what would that do? I poured a glass of apple juice and walked back into my room.

Loyal was knocked out by the time I made it back to my room. My eyes were locked on his sleeping face. There was something special about watching him sleep. Holding the apple juice I realized I had no idea what I was supposed to do. The only man who had ever slept in my bed was a gay guy friend Sam who didn't count. Sleeping in the bed with him was not going to happen. I wasn't ready to let him in on my snoring or my tossing and turning I did during the night. Blanket and pillow in hand I headed to my living room.

I nearly jumped out of my skin when I felt a hand on my shoulder. Loyal was standing over me still in his boxers and tee.

"What time is it?" I covered my mouth as I yawned in case I had morning breath.

"It's like five. I'm sorry, babe, I fell asleep. Your bed is comfortable as shit." Loyal sat on the edge of the couch. "Why didn't you just sleep with me?"

I shrugged my shoulders. "You looked so peaceful I didn't want to interrupt you."

Loyal laughed. He kissed me on my forehead. "This is why you are my Raynedrop." He held my hand as he stood up.

Loyal pulled me to my feet and I followed him to my bedroom. He pulled my robe off of me. For the first time I didn't feel uncomfortable as I climbed into bed with just a pair of boy shorts on. Loyal crawled into the bed next to me. We spooned. I hadn't spooned in years. Feeling his arms hugging me was perfection. I felt safe and wanted, all just from his touch.

Loyal kissed the back of my neck. Slowly he kissed down my spine stopping right above my ass. I turned over on my back as he kissed my stomach. Each delicate kiss felt different and new, like it was the first time. Loyal's fingers found their way between the cotton on my boy shorts. Lying there Loyal stuck his two middle fingers in me, slowly fingering me. My body jumped each time he hit my softest place.

We continued to kiss as he finger fucked me into an erotic oblivion. I couldn't fathom how a man could know how to hit spots just as well as any woman I had ever dated.

"Fuck me," I whispered in Loyal's ear.

He looked into my eyes.

"Fuck me, please."

Loyal continued to stare at me without stopping his assault on my vagina. He kissed my lips.

"No, Raynedrop," Loyal whispered back as I came on his hand. He pulled his fingers out and pushed them into my mouth. I sucked my sweetness off of his hand. I wanted more. I wanted to feel him inside of me. Why was he denying me what I wanted?

Loyal kissed me one more time before wrapping his arm back around me. Unable to look at him, I turned over on my side. Loyal pulled me so close to him I could feel his erection against my ass. Was he feeling the same torture he was dishing to me? I began to grind on his penis.

"Behave," Loyal laughed.

I wasn't ready to give up. I pulled his penis out of his boxers using my hand to slowly stroke it.

"Rayne . . ." Loyal smirked but didn't stop me.

I remembered how much he enjoyed my head the first time. I scooted down in my bed and began to suck his thickness. Loyal moaned as his hand massaged my scalp. Even if I didn't penetrate I knew this grade A head session would lead to me receiving some more of his amazing mouth action. I sucked his dick like I was working toward a prize, and I was.

As time passed I realized his hand wasn't massaging my head anymore. I looked up to find Loyal asleep like a baby. I didn't know if I was supposed to feel offended or not. I pulled away and his eyes opened.

"What?" he murmured.

"Well you were asleep so I figured I didn't need to continue." I rolled my eyes.

Loyal smiled. He motioned for me to come back to the head of the bed. He put his arms around me and kissed me on my cheek. In seconds he was asleep again. I knew there would be no waking him up again.

I heard water running in my bathroom as I woke up. The night before flashed in my head. I had fallen asleep with him. I jumped up and attempted to make myself look as good as I could before he came back in.

"Raynedrop," Loyal called as he walked back in my room. He was already completely dressed. "Thanks for taking care of my drunk ass last night."

I remembered the head I was giving him. "I guess," I said with attitude.

"What's wrong?" he replied picking up my attitude.

"You lied to me. You said I gave you good head but last night you fell asleep while I was doing it."

Loyal laughed. He walked up on me and put his hands on my shoulders. "Rayne, me falling asleep had nothing to do with your skills. I was tired and what you were doing was soothing so it helped me sleep. It isn't a bad thing."

"Really?" I was confused. I'd never experienced a person falling asleep during any type of sex before.

"Really, you ol' paranoid girl." Loyal kissed my forehead. "Trust me, I don't fall asleep at people's houses. I trust you enough to do so. It's a good thing. We are good."

I felt a warm feeling taking over my body. He was comfortable enough with me to do things he didn't do with all women. This revelation made me feel special. I didn't want him to leave but I knew I couldn't let on about just how happy I was. The last thing I wanted to do was scare him away.

Chapter 7

How I was able to act like nothing was happening between us, I wasn't sure. But there was fun in fooling everyone around us. Three weeks passed quicker than I ever imagined. I felt naughty at work. No one had a clue that there was anything going on between Loyal and myself. Yet they did notice that the influx of women over to his desk had subsided. Whenever he would walk away and come back Loyal would find some way to touch me, even if it was just a slight touch to the back of my neck.

Even with all the time we spent together we still never officially had sex. I was sure he had put some type of root on me because I not only sucked dick, but I loved doing it. I was content hearing him moan and feeling his hands against my head. I loved sucking his dick as much as I loved the taste of pussy in my mouth. He was no stranger to oral either. The man knew how to make my toes curl with the intensity of his tongue.

Most of the nights we spent together were with me giving him head or him fingering me until I came. He didn't give head like I wanted him to, but that was becoming a distant memory. I was growing restless. Not only was I not getting head but we still hadn't officially had sex. I wanted it all and I wanted it now.

Our area was quiet as our last coworker left for the night. As soon as the coast was clear I turned to him. "So there is this sushi place down the street that just opened up and I was thinking of having some sitting at my house later on tonight."

Loyal looked up from his cell phone. "Um, really, well I don't know about tonight."

I frowned. I wasn't used to getting a no, especially when food was involved.

"Is there a problem?" I questioned hoping I wasn't sounding like a jealous girlfriend.

"I have some plans but I'll call you."

Before I could respond he was back texting someone on his phone. A piece of me wanted to grab the phone and throw it in the trash. That was one thing that was starting to bother me about him. He was glued to his phone all while at work. When he came to my house it never rang, but while at work I would hear the vibrator going off every few minutes. I used the phone as the reminder not to like this man. He wasn't going to be more than what we were, and as long as I thought that every text was from a different woman I would never fall for him.

My eyes wouldn't focus. No matter how much I tried to work on my art my eyes kept shifting over to my phone. Loyal didn't call. It was the fourth night in a row that Loyal didn't call. I didn't even want sex anymore; I just wanted to feel his arms around me. If I didn't do something I was going to go insane. I picked up the phone and called his number.

He didn't answer.

A rush of emotion came over my body. I wasn't angry; I felt foolish. Laughter took over. I couldn't stop laughing. I was craving a man who I still hadn't physically slept with. The emotional girl in me was taking over my practical side and I knew I needed to put an end to that. My paintings were staring at me. All the paintings I'd created of strong women and I was standing in front of them acting like a little bitch over a man who owed me nothing.

My phone rang.

Loyal's face popped up. Before I had too much time to think about it I pressed the ignore button. The strong woman in me surfaced. I knew I couldn't continue to be available whenever he wanted me. I was going to need to set some boundaries for myself before things got completely out of control.

Chapter 8

The clicking of my heels was distracting me from my goal. I spent the night painting while coming up with my ultimate goal for what I wanted to happen between Loyal and myself. My master plan started with me dressing up again for work. My jeans were fitting in all the right places and my pink shirt hung down just enough to show off my breasts to anyone I chose to bend down in front of. I added accessories including jewelry, which I never wore. I wanted to make a statement.

"Rayne!"

I paused when I heard Camille's voice calling me. A piece of me wanted to keep walking. I didn't know if I was up to the questions about who I was dressing up for or the criticism for whatever makeup I was missing.

Camille finished up her call and went into a break mode so she wouldn't get any more. "You look cute, girl." Camille began to rummage through the suitcase she called a purse. She pulled out a compact of eye shadow colors.

"What are you doing?"

"I'm fixing your makeup." She started checking the tones to see what she wanted to use. A piece of me wanted to resist, but I knew she could only help the situation.

I closed my eyes as Camille applied various colors on my face. The brush felt funny as she pressed down on my eyelid. "What colors are you using?"

"I ask the questions around here, ma'am," Camille said.

She continued for a few more moments before telling me to open my eyes. My mouth dropped open. My eyes looked amazing.

"Here." Camille handed me a pink gloss, which added the last bit of elegance to my new look.

"Thanks, I actually look cute." I began to gather my things.

"Yeah. I'm sure Loyal is going to love it."

Camille's statement caused me to freeze in my spot. My face jerked around toward Camille, who had a very devilish grin on her face.

"What?"

"Girl, please, it's so obvious with your half-gay ass." Camille giggled.

I immediately sat back in the chair. "What do you mean? There is nothing going on—"

"Girl, save that for someone who doesn't know you. I see the way you look at him. You never come over anymore; you are always just kicking it with him. Not to mention whenever you are around him you have straight googly eyes."

"I do not."

"Really? Hold on. Larry!"

Before I could object Camille had called her supervisor Larry over to the desk. Larry walked over sporting his usual black. I didn't know a man could own nothing but black and gray but he literally wore black and gray every day.

"What's going on?" Larry put his hand on my shoulder. "You look cute, Rayne."

"Larry, why do you think she put on makeup?"

Larry looked at me and smiled. "I'm guessing it's for pretty Ricky over in your bay."

Camille and Larry started laughing. I was mortified. "Why would you say that?"

Larry's upper lip curled. He folded his arms. "Girl, you be looking at him like you want to sop him up with some gravy and a biscuit."

They continued to laugh at my expense before Larry was called off by a new hire needing his help. I wanted to die. "Camille, seriously is it that obvious?"

"That you like him? Yeah, it's pretty obvious. Wait, you aren't actually messing with him are you?"

"Ugh no." I frowned. I couldn't tell her the truth or anyone else.

"I was about to say. I mean I don't have a problem with you getting some dick but don't get the community dick."

"Community dick?"

"Hell yeah, that dick belongs to the call center. It's no telling how many girls he's already slept with. Dude ain't been here no time at all and I've already heard he's knocking off like four different chicks in customer service and authorizations."

I didn't like what I was hearing but I kept a straight face. Could he really be sleeping with that many other women at our job? I knew girls came over to the desk a lot but I always figured they were trying to get with him, not actually sleeping with him.

"So you are sitting here telling me that you don't care if I'm sleeping with a man just as long as it's not him? What the fuck?"

Camille sat forward in her chair. She looked around to make sure no one was paying attention to us. "Look, bitch, yo' ass hasn't been with anyone since I met you so no, at this point I don't care if it's dick or pussy just get you some."

I nodded my head. "I really didn't expect that response but let me go to my desk on that note."

All my belongings in tow, I headed to my desk where Loyal was already sitting talking to our coworkers. His eyes widened with the rest of them.

"Oh shit Rayne must have a big date tonight." Loyal's grin wasn't cute today; it was rather annoying.

"*Bonita,*" Rosalyn added.

I thanked them all while trying to ignore Loyal who wouldn't stop smiling at me.

"So who you getting all cute for today, Rayne?" Loyal's smug voice only infuriated me. I decided two could play at this game.

"I have a date tonight."

Before I could finish my sentence all my fellow coworkers were staring at me. The questions of who, what, when, and where came flooding in. Loyal sat at his desk just watching the interrogation with the same devilish smile on his face.

I created a whole story in my head. I was having dinner with a fellow artist in the showcase. He had flirted with me a few times but I just finally decided to take him up on the offer. Loyal's facial expressions never changed. He didn't seem to care at all about this mystery artist I was going out with. I knew I was going to have to think of something better to get his attention. Once the scene had died down I decided to go in for the kill.

"So do you think it would be wrong to invite him to see my studio?" I kept the straightest face I could muster.

Loyal turned around with a normal, professional look on his face. "I don't see why not. You are both artists; maybe he can give you some pointers or something," Loyal said, quickly turning back to his desk.

"Okay." I didn't know what to say. He didn't seem to care at all. I didn't have another card to play. There were no more cards for me to play. Defeated I turned back to my desk and began my workday.

I was ready for the night to be over. The days of us laughing and joking at work were a thing of the past. Now

he barely spoke to me unless other people were present,
No longer did he stay at this desk on his break, now he
disappeared, always with his cell phone planted firmly in
his hand. I could understand why some women went so
crazy when it came to men's cellphones. Every time he
ignored me to check his phone or send a text I wanted to
throw his phone out of a window.

I began to pack my things up for the night. A piece of
me wanted to call him out on his bad behavior but I knew
that would get me nowhere.

"Have fun on your date." Loyal winked his eye before
walking out of the office. He left me there dumbfounded.

Home never felt so lonely. I didn't want to be alone,
but I couldn't bring myself to call Loyal and tell him that
everything was made up. Maybe I could lie and tell him
the date got canceled. The truth was I didn't want to be
with anyone else.

My phone rang the moment I walked into the door.
Loyal's face popped up on the screen.

"Yes," I answered as quickly as I could.

"Aren't you supposed to be on a date?"

Loyal's smooth voice only made it harder for me to lie
to him. I swallowed the knot forming in my throat. "Why
does it matter to you?"

There was a brief silence on the line. I heard a knock
at my front door. My body froze. I gained composure
enough to walk to the door. I didn't need to look in the
peephole. I could feel him through the door. I exhaled
and opened the door.

"For the record, you going on a date is something I
will never get upset about. However, you lying to me to
attempt to make me jealous is something that will piss
me off."

Loyal walked past me and into my house. I closed the door behind him, not saying a word. We made it into my studio. He focused on the sculpture that had changed drastically since the last time he had seen it.

"Loyal, what are you doing here?"

"Why did you lie to me?" He didn't turn away from the sculpture.

"Because maybe I'm tired of you feeling like you are the only one who can please me. You treat me like I'm some random chick you can come run in and run out on like I'm not shit. You treat these bitches at work better than you treat my ass."

"What makes you say that?" Loyal asked as he finally turned toward me.

"Loyal, I'm not stupid. You barely talk to me at work. You are always texting on your phone. You ignore me and you haven't been over here in a while. And you still haven't tried to sleep with me."

Loyal listened to my rant without taking his eyes off of me. I couldn't turn it off. I continued to go off. I questioned why it was okay to do certain things with me but not give me the full package the other women received. I knew I sounded crazy but I didn't care. I wanted him and he needed to know it.

"Rayne."

"What!"

"Rayne." Loyal walked closer to me with the same calm manner he used to call my name. He took my hands, holding them in his own. "Rayne, I told you from day one I wasn't going to sleep with you."

I pulled away. "That doesn't make any fucking sense. I can give you head and we can do all we do but you can't give me any penis?"

The fact that I was even asking for penis sounded strange coming out of my mouth. Loyal couldn't help but laugh. "Rayne, you are supposed to be a lesbian right?"

"Fuck you, Loyal. That lesbian ship sank the moment I put my mouth on yo' ass."

"Raynedrop, you know you are my girl right? You are my friend. I mean I really consider you a friend. You are one of the only women I totally trust. I am not about to mess that up by sleeping with you. I know what happens when I sleep with women."

"Oh, cocky nigga, I don't give a damn about your penis. There isn't enough penis in the world that will make me go that crazy," I said as I rolled my neck and crossed my arms.

"That's what your mouth says."

We once again had hit a wall and neither one of us had intentions of backing down. This man was driving me insane, yet I couldn't stay away. My mind raced as we stood there as though we were about to duel. I wasn't giving up. I couldn't.

"What am I doing? What are we doing?" I threw my hands in the air, turned, and walked away. I could hear Loyal following me.

"Rayne . . ."

"Loyal, just go."

"Don't be like that." Loyal attempted to walk close but was met by my hand.

"Loyal, you know what? This is some bullshit and you know it. You can come over here, do whatever you want and I allow you to do it. But when I want something I'm constantly met with a no. But I get it. You don't have to do a damn thing because there are others you have waiting for the phone call. Well you know what, go ahead. Make your phone calls; just erase my number while you are at it."

Loyal let out a deep growl as he paced the floor while rubbing his bald head. He was frustrated. I didn't care. I wanted him to feel the frustration he put me through on a daily basis. He continued to pace the floor letting out a grunt or mumble every few moments. I stood there with my arms folded. I didn't care that I was upsetting him; I had been upset for months. Loyal turned one more time toward me, standing still in his position.

"Rayne, you are so fucking difficult. I'm sitting here trying to save you from your damn self but you just want to fucking fall don't you?"

"Nigga—"

"No wait!" This time Loyal's hand was up. "You asking for something and you have absolutely no idea what you are doing. Some of the bitches I fuck with are sluts; they fuck and they fuck a lot. And you know what, they are still strung the fuck out over Loyal. You want to know what would happen if I gave your naive ass what you are asking for?"

I couldn't move. Loyal rushed up on me. He pulled my arm, causing my body to jerk toward him. This wasn't sweet or sensual; it was completely primal.

"If I fuck you, Rayne, you would never leave me alone. I could dog the shit out of you and you would still answer my calls whenever I called. Is that what you want? You want me to own you? Because if I fuck you, I will. Is that what you want?"

My bottom lip trembled along with the rest of my body. He had never talked to me like that and for the first time I actually believed every word that came out of his mouth. I couldn't help but wonder if it really was that serious. Loyal didn't take his eyes off me. Out of all the emotions I'd ever felt for him, this was the first time I felt fear. I was scared that everything he was saying could possibly come true; yet my body still yearned for him.

"Loyal, until you walked into that office I was content with what I was. But you have opened up something in me that needs more. I hear what you are saying, but I don't care. I need to experience pleasure, and I need to experience it with you. This shit I'm feeling isn't going away. That itch, you have to scratch it. I need you to."

I knew I laid the gauntlet and was eager to know his response. Loyal shook his head from side to side, over and over again. "Rayne, you don't really know what you are asking."

"Yes, I do." Our eyes met again.

This time I did the pulling. I pulled Loyal's shirt causing his body to crash into mine. Nothing else mattered. I had never wanted anyone so bad before in my life. I no longer had control of my body. Even without giving it to him, he already owned me.

Loyal lowered his head. He pushed my head up with his finger until our eyes met. "Rayne, you need to understand, I will never be the boyfriend. There is nothing that you will ever do or say that will change that."

I tried to interrupt but Loyal covered my mouth with his hand.

"Now, if I do decide to give you what you want, you are going to have to remember what I just said to you. I can take you to heaven, but if you fall for me, trust me it will be worse than hell for you. I am not going to settle down, not with you or anyone else."

Loyal's hands rubbed up and down my arms. I could see his lips were moving but I couldn't comprehend what he was saying. I didn't want to hear another word. I just wanted to feel him next to me.

There wasn't anything else I could say. Either he was going to take me or leave me. I felt like I needed to say something more, maybe one more thing to solidify what I was trying to make him understand. With every bit of energy left in me, I formed my lips for one more plea.

"Please me . . ."

Chapter 9

I could feel his chest rumble when he let out another deep groan. In one fell swoop I was off the floor and in his arms. I was already shocked. I knew he was buff, but never in a million years did I think this man could actually pick me up.

Loyal carried me over to the couch in my studio space. He laid me down on my back. I watched as he unbuttoned each button on his white shirt. One by one each piece of his clothing came off. He laid everything nice and neat on the chair in the corner.

Loyal went into his pocket. He pulled something out but I couldn't tell what it was. He walked back over to me. With his hand on the back of my head I took his manhood in my mouth. He wasn't nearly as hard as I knew he could get. I knew how to fix that. My mouth consumed his dick, reaching to the back of my throat. I sucked, allowing the tip of my tongue to dance all over his thickness. I could feel him growing in my mouth. Before long it wasn't able to reach as far as it was to begin with.

Loyal pulled his penis out and I watched as he placed a condom on his shaft. Suddenly things were real. We weren't just giving each other head, this was really about to happen. My body began to tense up. My nerves were trying to get the best of me. Everything I just said to him was going out the window. I wasn't ready. I didn't know what made me think I was.

Before I could object Loyal flipped my body over. He pulled my legs off of the couch. Standing there with my belly lying against the couch and my ass in the air I knew I had to do something to stop this.

It was too late.

I felt the tip of Loyal's man touch the outer crevice of my pussy. I wasn't ready. If we had a safe word I would have yelled it at the top of my lungs. For some reason I couldn't speak. I bit my lip, closed my eyes and prepared for the inevitable.

Pain.

A sharp pain pierced my body as Loyal's penis entered me. My mouth dropped open. Loyal held the sides of my thighs. He didn't move or stroke, he just let the tip become familiar with the entrance of my cave.

"Relax."

I held on to his hand as I attempted to follow directions. I felt like I was a virgin all over again, experiencing the first touch all over again. Within a moment Loyal slowly began to push his manhood deeper inside of me.

The pain continued to pierce me with every inch of movement. I wasn't going to be able to take this. It was everything I remembered, painful and uncomfortable. I was going to have to tell him to stop. I felt like a fool. I practically begged him to give it to me and I was giving up without a full stroke completed.

"Loy—"

Suddenly everything changed. Loyal slowly pulled back. A tidal wave of my essence came flooding down washing the pain away and turning it into a titillating heat that covered every inch of my body.

"Damn, girl," Loyal said feeling the massive wetness covering him. "You really did need some."

I couldn't be embarrassed; nothing mattered. I needed to feel that warmth again. Loyal obliged pushing back inside of me causing the heat to rise again. With each stroke I felt my body giving in to Loyal's every whim. I felt my body trembling with each move.

I closed my eyes, trying to hold in the moans that wanted to escape my mouth. Even with my eyes closed I could see a kaleidoscope of colors dancing in front of me. He worked his magic causing every inch of my body to radiate with ecstasy. I could feel him in my toes, my caves, and inching up my thighs. This wasn't anything I had experienced before.

Loyal's hands gripped my sides and with force he let out a grunt as he pushed deep inside touching a spot I didn't know existed. I couldn't hold it in. A loud moan escaped my lips and echoed through my art space. He didn't pull back. Loyal allowed his manhood to linger at my softest spot. Slowly he pushed deeper, pushing my button over and over. The intensity now reached from my thighs up into my stomach. I got what it meant when women said they could feel it in their stomach.

"Turn around." Loyal whispered as his man finally left the inner depths of me.

I wasn't sure if I could walk. I tried to turn only causing my ass to crash down on my couch. Before I could catch my breath Loyal had my shirt over my head. I sat there naked in only my bra. I let him remove the bra from me. I was comfortable with him seeing me. He was the only person who had ever seen me completely naked.

Loyal's lips met my right nipple as he squeezed my left nipple with his thick fingers. He pulled my legs apart, entering me without taking his mouth off me. My bottom lip quivered as the tip of his dick pushed deep inside. He pushed my legs up to the sky as I held on to his arms. It wasn't slow this time. He pushed in and out with quickness, tapping my spot with each stroke. Each time he hit my place I felt like my heart was going to jump right out of my chest.

I closed my eyes and let Loyal take my body on the wildest ride imaginable. I never felt so good. My body trembled with every touch, grind, and lick. My massive breasts jumped with every stroke, hitting my chin until I finally grabbed them. I massaged my own breasts as Loyal continued the assault on my body. I knew my neighbors had to hear me, but I didn't care. I wanted the whole world to experience what I felt in that very moment.

Now familiar with my flexibility, Loyal used it to his advantage. My legs reached new heights and widths as we left the couch for the cold hardwood floor. We didn't care as he turned me into various positions all over the bare floor. Even I was amazed at the various positions my big body was able to contort into for him.

I felt a familiar ball forming in the pit of my stomach. I braced myself for what I knew was about to come. But he stopped. Loyal pulled out and patted me on my side. As my eyes focused I noticed he was motioning for me to turn back over. I slowly forced my body back up. As I turned my eyes noticed the clock, we had been going at it for over an hour and I didn't even realize it.

Loyal disappeared. I turned to see my bathroom light on. Moments later he appeared holding a small bottle. I knew that bottle; it was from my goodie bag of condoms, lube, and dental dam I acquired while at Memphis Gay Pride.

Loyal had me stand on the side of the couch. I bent over, resting my elbows on my couch cushion. I jumped when I felt him pulling my ass cheeks open.

"Wait!" I jumped. I knew ass play was not on the menu.

"Relax." Loyal's deep voice echoed through the room.

I knew this was a bad idea. I could barely take the punishment he gave to my pussy. I knew my untouched ass was not ready for anything. My protests fell on deaf ears.

"You asked for it, so I'm giving it to you. So like I said, relax."

Loyal's stern voice made me want to obey. I closed my eyes. My whole body tensed up the moment I felt the wet tip of his penis touch my rim. Loyal rubbed his hands against my body.

"You gotta relax," he repeated as the tip of his dick grazed my asshole.

I knew it was now or never. With a deep breath I felt the tip enter my ass. I exhaled as he slowly entered me. Loyal slowly pushed farther inside of me. I was waiting for the pain, but it never came. The moment he began to extract back I felt a new level of heat covering my body. This was the most pleasurable feeling I'd ever felt.

I wanted more. I moaned for more. Loyal pushed my body down on the couch. He told me to get on my stomach and I quickly listened. Before long his man found home in my ass, stroking me like he had lived there his whole life.

This wasn't normal. The normal tingling sensations were heightened by 100 percent. I didn't have a ball forming in my stomach; it was a fucking massive explosion. My body betrayed me as it convulsed uncontrollably. I wanted to yell his name but I couldn't form words. Only small breaths and high-pitched squeals left my mouth. I balled my hand into a fist as I felt my body about to explode. I couldn't stop my hand from pounding my couch over and over as death not only approached but killed my ass. As soon as I thought it was over another rush took over as I died another thousand little deaths. I couldn't breathe. I had no control over my own body. No less than three minutes later another hot splash took over causing me to flood all over my couch.

Loyal slowly pulled out. I was spent. He stood up, walking toward me. I looked up at him. He pulled the condom off and pulled my arms until I was sitting up.

Loyal pushed his penis in my mouth and I gladly accepted it. I could taste the latex but I didn't care. I sucked his dick while he jerked it with his left hand. I heard him moan until his moan turned into a groan. His voice trembled as he grabbed my ponytail causing my neck to fall back. He let out a loud moan that made his whole body tremble as his babies covered lips, chin, and rolled down my neck.

He had never cum before, and no one had ever cum on me before. Loyal walked off to the bathroom leaving me covered in the room. I wasn't sure what I was supposed to do. Curiosity was killing me. I opened my tightly closed lips allowing some of Loyal's essence to spill into my mouth. Something I always figured would be horrific was the opposite. It was sweeter than I ever expected.

After two failed attempts of standing up I finally gained my composure. Holding on to the wall I walked toward the bathroom. I saw Loyal standing naked in front of my sink. He turned around and smiled. He covered one of my washcloths with warm water. I walked close as Loyal began to wipe his essence off of my body. He kissed my lips.

"You okay?"

I still couldn't speak so I simply nodded my head.

We walked back into my art space and turned the light on. We erupted in laughter when we saw the large wet stain on my couch. I was shocked. I had no idea I could cause anything of the sort.

I put my robe on while I watched Loyal dress. He picked up his clothes that he carefully laid down before we started. There wasn't a wrinkle in sight. I walked him to the door. I wanted to tell him to stay just to make the night perfect, but I knew that wasn't an option. Loyal put his hands on both sides of my face. He looked me directly in my eyes.

"You aren't going to change on me are you?" Loyal asked in his usual calm tone.

I shook my head no. Loyal's lips planted firmly against my forehead. He winked his right eye before walking out of my door. I closed the door behind him. I stood in the hallway for a moment. I didn't know what I was feeling, as I had never felt anything like it before. I heard one of my clocks chime. I was amazed when I realized we were going at it for over two and a half hours. From what I remembered about men it usually only lasted about fifteen minutes; an hour was impossible.

That moment I felt him inside of me again causing my legs to buckle. I caught myself by holding the side of the wall. The aftershocks were just as intense as the earthquake he put on me. I somehow made it to my bed. I didn't make it under the covers. I stared at my roof until my eyes were too heavy to stay open. I welcomed sleep. I just hoped pleasant dreams would come with it.

Chapter 10

The bright light shining in my window hurt my sensitive morning eyes. I covered them as I sat up in my bed. The night quickly came back to me as I didn't have my usual comforter to pull off of me. I could still feel the ache of sex in my womanhood.

I ran my hot shower. I didn't care about covering my hair. I stepped into the steam, closed my eyes, and let the hot water take me back to the night before. I could smell his cologne, feel his hands on my body, and his lips against mine. I touched my stomach as butterflies fluttered around.

My body felt rejuvenated like I had spent a weekend at a spa. My body was looser than I remembered. I felt like I'd attended a massive session of yoga, which wasn't too far off when I remembered all the positions Loyal had me in the night before.

Looking at myself in the mirror I didn't see any difference but I sure felt it. Everything in my world had changed overnight. I not only had sex with a man, but I loved every moment of it. Everything I thought I'd known was different. I was crazy about a man, something I never imagined would happen.

Bruno Mars was ringing from my phone. I didn't want to be disturbed but something told me I should check it. I made it back to my room just as it stopped ringing. I checked the ID to see Bianca's face on my screen. I pressed redial.

"You are a horrible best friend and I am disowning you."

Bianca's voice echoed through my speaker phone. I set the phone on the bathroom sink and started my morning beauty routine. "Sorry, hon, a lot has been happening." I smiled thinking about Loyal.

"I bet. I haven't talked to you in ages. Still having slumber parties with the Mexican?"

I could picture Bianca's eyes rolling while she made the snide comment.

"Whatever." I rolled my eyes. I wanted to tell my friend about my night, but I wasn't ready to. My mind was still racing and I hadn't fully processed everything yet. I listened to Bianca talk about her wedding dress and how wonderful the new dress was starting to look. I zoned out during talks of flowers and décor. I had other things to think about besides her wedding.

"So do you need me to come early to the show or are you going to need any help getting your stuff to the gallery?"

I had moved from the bathroom to my kitchen during wedding talk. I sat at the table with my mouth wide open. I looked over at the calendar. The biggest show in my career was approaching in a few weeks.

"Rayne?"

"I am fucked." I spit my toast out and grabbed the phone. I walked into my art space. I could still see the wet spot on my couch.

"What are you talking about?" Bianca paused in her tracks. "Rayne, what is going on?"

"I just need to get back on the ball."

"Rayne, have you let this man come in between you and your work?"

I didn't want to answer the question. I knew the answer and I felt sick thinking about it.

"Rayne, don't tell me you are dickmatized." Bianca sat on an expensive leather chaise. "You can't be over there letting some dick fuck with all you have worked on."

"I know."

"Well act like that. Hell he hasn't even fucked you and you are already messing up. I need you to get yo' life, honey."

I hung up from Bianca and immediately called out for the day at work. I knew it was a good idea. I wasn't ready to see Loyal and I needed to get a full day of work in. I'd let a person come in and sidetrack me from my goal. There was a reason I cut myself off in the beginning and with the entrance of Loyal in my life I had broken all of my own rules. I knew I had to get things in order.

I let my paintbrush talk on an empty canvas. My usual color scheme was out the window. I could only concentrate on the color blue. I put my iPod on the dock and let the music move my soul and my paintbrush. I created a blue color that was borderline gray. I didn't know what was going to come from it, if anything, but my creative side was bursting at the seams.

Day became night before I knew it. In one day I had accomplished more than I had done in weeks. I put the final touches on three pieces I had been working on and my new blue painting was taking shape. My mind was being drawn to the sculpture that was under a sheet draped on it. I stared at the sheet not wanting to remove it. Suddenly I realized the whole day had gone by and Loyal hadn't called or texted me. I knew he was at work, but felt a twinge of anger that he didn't think to check on the person he had just slept with for the first time the night before.

I pulled the sheet off of the sculpture and stared at it. This was my reality and I knew it. Those hands had a hold of me and the one thing I had to hold on to was also now gone. I could hear his voice in my head. Did I really belong to him now? I shook my head. I wasn't going to allow myself to belong to anyone, especially not a man-whore like Loyal.

With my work on my mind I knew it was time to finish the sculpture. I threw on my jacket and headed to the large art supply store in my neighborhood.

"Hey, Rayne, long time." Jared, the owner, stood up as I walked into the building. Everything about Jared let you know he was an artist. His stringy jet-black hair hung on his shoulders giving off an earthy, beatnik vibe. His long, lanky body seemed to glide rather than walk as he came from behind the counter to greet me.

"Hey, Jared, what's that you're working on?" I pointed at a house he was painting on a canvas behind the counter.

Jared shrugged his shoulders. He started some mystical experience at the grocery store that had led him to think about the house he grew up in as a child. Jared never just painted because he wanted to. There always had to be some type of magical force that brought him to paint. As much as I thought he was crazy, I could only wish I had as much passion when I discussed my art.

"So what can I get for you today?" Jared held his hands together as he stared at me.

"I need to create a bronze for a sculpture."

"Sculpting. Very cool. I didn't know you were going to put a sculpture in the show." Jared glided toward the acrylic paints as I followed.

"I didn't know either. It just sorta came to me."

Jared stopped mid-walk and turned back to me. His eyes widened. "It just came to you?"

"Yeah."

"Yeah!" Jared clapped his hands together. "See I told you. The universe is going to guide you to what you need; you just have to open up, listen, and let it do the rest."

***

On the way home I couldn't stop thinking about Jared's words. Was my crazy friend right? Was the universe or something trying to tell me to mess with Loyal? I felt his presence before I ever met him. Was this an act of God or some powerful being? I shook my head knowing I had allowed myself to enter the crazy artist town that Jared lived in.

I picked up my phone only to see I still had no missed calls. If the universe did bring Loyal to me then it was one fucked-up universe. Why bring someone who would never be anything more than just a causal fling into my life?

I mixed the paint creating the perfect bronze that I wanted. I began to paint the first coat on the clay that I finally allowed to completely dry. The color was quickly bringing the sculpture to life from the dull gray of the clay. An hour later the first coat was complete. I took a step back and marveled at the difference the paint made. I couldn't smile. As beautiful and proud of my work as I was, the thought of Loyal and my situation haunted me. Why hadn't he called? Why did I care so much?

My body was aching from standing all day. I sat on my couch and felt an electric current pulse through my mind. I was back in his arms and I could feel him inside of me. I closed my eyes and leaned back on the couch. My mind drifted back to the night before. I could feel my body starting to heat up in anticipation. I didn't need him, but I wanted him and I knew the feeling wasn't going away anytime soon.

Chapter 11

My heart felt like it was going to jump out of my chest as I walked into the office. I could see his bald head out of my periphery. I knew I needed a moment before going to my desk. I saw Camille standing by the copy machine.

"What's up, *chica?*" I rushed over to her as quickly as I could.

"Girl, ready to go the hell home, I haven't gotten a sale all day." Camille rolled her eyes. "Where were you yesterday?"

"Working. The show is in a few weeks ya know."

"Yeah, I know. Hell I thought you were working Loyal's ass or something."

Her statement mortified me. Camille laughed. "Shit since neither one of y'all asses was at work yesterday I figured y'all were together."

I was shocked as I followed her back to her desk. My mind was racing with questions but I didn't want to seem obvious. I decided not to mention him at all. I changed the subject to my art show hoping she wouldn't be able to tell my real intentions.

I finally made it over to my area to find everyone already on phone calls with customers. Loyal didn't look at me like he usually did. I tried to ignore him as I settled into my desk. The air kicked on causing me to get a whiff of his cologne. My pussy twitched just from the familiar scent.

"What's up, Rayne?" Loyal said as he hung up with his caller. "You all right?"

"I'm good." I forced the words out of my mouth. I wanted to ask him where he was the other day but before I could say anything I heard Kyle call my name. We both turned to see Kyle walking up with a large smile on his face.

"Look what I got." Kyle held up a ticket to my art exhibit. "I got it yesterday after work when they said they were on sale. I know you really can't sell stuff up here at work."

"Thanks, Kyle, but you know I could have given you one."

Kyle shook his head. "No, I want to support you. Hey, Loyal, are you coming to the opening?"

"I wasn't invited." Loyal looked at me.

"Everyone is invited," I snapped back. His devilish grin was making my blood boil.

"In that case, maybe." Loyal turned back toward his desk.

The day was busier than I'd seen in a while. There wasn't much time for sitting around. On breaks Loyal disappeared like usual leaving us no time to discuss anything. I was happy when the end of our shift finally came to a close. I quickly packed my things up. For once I had no desire to actually speak to him about anything.

"You just gon' leave?" Loyal's voice echoed.

"I need to get home." I put my backpack on and grabbed my paperwork to turn in.

"What's the rush?"

Suddenly I felt my blood starting to boil again. I walked close to him. "The rush is I have an art opening in three weeks and I am behind because I allowed myself to be sidetracked by someone who doesn't even seem to care."

"Whoa. Are you serious right now? I don't care about your work?" Loyal grabbed my arm. "That's a low blow."
"Well if the shoe fits." I pulled away and walked away. I wasn't surprised that he didn't follow me.

I made it home and slammed the door. I didn't know why I was so angry but I couldn't help it. I pulled my work shirt and pants off and changed into one of my art smocks. I headed into my studio and turned on my iPod to my rock playlist. Paramore's Hayley Williams began to scream through the speakers.

I started working on the second coat for the sculpture. I banged my head along with the beat from the song. I turned around to re-dip my brush.

"Fuck!"

I jumped causing my foot to hit the paint canister, knocking it over on the floor. Loyal jumped standing in my doorway.

"What the fuck!" I noticed the paint flowing on the floor. I scrambled to try to salvage as much of the expensive paint as possible. Loyal disappeared and reappeared with a wet towel in his hands. He met me on the floor and started cleaning up the mess.

"I didn't mean to scare you. Did you know your door was open?"

"No," I snapped. "You don't just walk in and scare a person like that."

"You don't just leave your damn door open for anyone to come in. What if it would have been someone besides me?"

Loyal's and my eyes met. I felt my hands trembling. "What are you doing here?" I poured the paint I was able to catch on paper back into the can.

"Well seems like you had some shit you wanted to say at work and I knew that wasn't the place for it so I just decided to come on over so you could say it."

I sighed. "Loyal, it was nothing. I'm just stressed. I got a lot going on."

"No, it's something. You don't just say I don't care about your work and not mean it." Loyal sat on my stool without taking his eyes off of me.

"Look I just didn't realize how much work I have to do in the next weeks. Not to mention I have press and photo shoots and more and I am not done."

"And it's my fault you haven't been doing your work?" Loyal crossed his arms.

"I didn't say that."

"But you implied it."

"I just really need to get back on the ball. This is my dream. I can't let it pass because I got involved with anyone."

Loyal nodded his head. He stood up and pulled his shirt over his head. I couldn't help but stare at his beautiful arms in his undershirt. "All right, what can I do?"

I watched him lay his shirt down as perfectly as he always did.

"Are you serious?"

"I mean I know I'm no artist but if you are just putting a coat of paint on that I think I can handle it."

If I wasn't watching I wouldn't have believed it. Loyal helped me finish the second coat on the sculpture. Just like always he was very thorough, paying attention to every stoke making it the best he could. We finished the coat quickly.

I watched Loyal wash his hands in my bathroom. I couldn't stop smiling. He actually cared enough to help me with my work. Loyal looked at me through the reflection in the mirror.

"What are you looking at?"

I didn't know what came over me. I walked in the bathroom and stood behind him. Loyal turned around and I immediately began to unbutton his pants. He asked what I thought I was doing. I didn't respond. I pulled his pants down and dropped to my knees.

Loyal closed his eyes as I worked my mouth around his penis. I felt him swell in my mouth. A feeling of determination swept over my body. I wanted to please him more than I'd ever wanted to please him before. My tongue rolled around his tip as my hand moved in unison with my mouth around his shaft. He put both of his hands on my head pushing me as deep as I could go. I sucked until I gagged slightly. Loyal told me to stand up. He grabbed my Pride goodie bag and headed to my bedroom.

Loyal pushed me over the side of my bed. He pulled my art smock up and pulled my boy shorts off quickly. In a moment he had a condom on and was inside of me. I bit my bottom lip as he fucked me senseless. Loyal grabbed my hair as he put one of his feet on top of my bed. My mouth dropped open as he began to pound me. This was different from the night before. There was nothing sensual or romantic. He was straight fucking me.

I couldn't moan. I whimpered as I became his bitch. He grunted with every pound. His dick didn't press my button; it punched it with full force causing me to let out a short screech with each touch. Loyal pulled out long enough to throw me on my back. He pushed my legs in the air and began his assault missionary style. I tried to look at him but he was in a different world. He wasn't looking at me; he was looking through me.

I didn't like it, but my body quickly betrayed me. I felt my whole body tensing up and the newly familiar balls forming in my stomach. This wasn't the orgasm I had the night before. Just like his sex my orgasm hit me like a wild animal attacking its prey. My body convulsed, jerking and trembling.

Loyal ignored my orgasm as his own was on the horizon. He let out a loud growl as he came. He dropped down on top of me; the sweat from his head covered my stomach. Loyal stood up and quickly disappeared to the bathroom leaving me utterly confused, frozen in the spot he left me in.

I didn't move. I was still dumbfounded by the assault that just happened on my body, and another part of me wondered was he coming back for a second round. To my surprise Loyal walked back to the door completely dressed as though nothing had happened. I sat up on the bed looking at him with pure confusion.

"Well I gotta bounce. I'll talk to you later, Raynedrop."

With a wink and smirk he was gone.

Chapter 12

I stood next to the other artists in the show while the photographer snapped picture after picture of us. Bianca stood in the background attempting to guide my movements for the shoot. I felt out of place next to the artists. They truly had a diverse group. Paulo was a Hispanic industrial designer with long dark hair. He looked like he belonged on the cover of a Harlequin romance novel with Amber, a painter with the usual beautiful blond hair and deep blue eyes. Opie was my favorite; he was a total nerd wearing bifocals and who was obviously socially awkward but made up for it in his art. Pashun was the resident hippie artist who didn't use his real name, wore baggy clothes and long, thick locks, and seemed to never wear shoes.

They finally called for break, which was greatly appreciated. I knew I looked great but the shoes Bianca had me in were killing my feet and I was afraid to walk in them. I pulled the shoes off the moment they called for the break.

"Rayne, how are you, love?" Pashun walked over to me. It was obvious he had a thing for me. He knew I was gay but that never seemed to stop him from trying. My current situation flashed in my mind. How things could change in the course of a few months.

"Pashun, I'm great, how are you?"

He gave me a hug. I knew Bianca was cringing at the sight. She always felt like he had to be dirty because of the way he dressed. I knew him to be different. He looked like a struggling artist but was quite the opposite. Pashun had sold many paintings and was living off his own wealth in a gorgeous downtown loft he also used as his studio space.

"Great. I hear you are showing a sculpture. Nice."

"Yeah, it just kinda came out of nowhere."

"Things don't appear out of nowhere; it was in you all along, mama." He smiled.

I smiled back. He wasn't ugly by far, which was one of the reasons he never had a problem in the area of women. Pashun was admired for his beauty and the beauty he created with his paintbrush. He also was a poet, which only made the panties drop faster for him. Even with the appeal I just wasn't attracted to him in the way he wanted me to be.

"So are you ready for the show?" I said hoping to take the spotlight off of myself.

Pashun nodded his head. "I'm not taking this show so seriously ya know. I'd honestly rather see someone like you get the job. I thought about backing out. I don't like the idea of art being a contest. It's about love you know, not competition."

Pashun placed his slender hands on my shoulders. He slowly massaged my shoulder with his hand. I wanted to laugh but held my composure.

"So you should let me roll through, Rayne, and check your work out. I'm willing to help out if you need it."

"I'm actually great. I have one more coat to put on the sculpture and some buffing and I'm done. My paintings are all finished. But thank you."

Pashun smiled. He slowly shook his head. "Rayne, you are so mysterious. You should let someone in sometimes. It can be liberating."

Just then I was saved by a photographer calling Pashun's name. He bowed his head and walked away to join the photographer and interviewer. Bianca appeared seconds after his departure with the usual frown she wore whenever she saw him.

"Ugh I thought he would never leave." Bianca typed away on her phone. "So the photographer is going to take a few more photos of you—"

"I slept with Loyal."

The revelation made Bianca look up from her phone. I didn't know what came over me but I had to tell someone.

"I slept with him, it was amazing, and I slept with him again after that, and now it's five days later and I haven't heard from him. Not a text, a phone call, nothing."

Bianca threw her phone in her purse and put hands on each of my shoulders. "Okay so yeah, shocker but it's okay. You got some . . . from a man . . . Okay. Okay. That's fine. It's normal for them not to call right after. You probably needed a little time away from him."

"I think I made a big mistake. I let this man pretty much change everything about me. I don't really know who I am right now. My whole life I have been gay. And now, now I don't know what I am."

The revelation was hard but true. Every night I sat up wondering about my life. Was I ever really gay? I knew I had loved my ex, but this feeling I had now was completely different and much more intense. I was attracted to women and never found myself attracted to men. I could feel myself becoming overcome with emotions. I felt Bianca grab my hand and pull me to the side. She turned toward me, looking directly into my face.

"Ok sweetie I love you but now is not the time for this. Yes, you got yourself in a little pickle but right now you have to be amazing artist not confused chick. So snap out of it. We will figure out your love life after you are done taking over the Memphis art scene."

I knew she was right. I took a deep breath and sucked in the emotions trying to take over my mind at that moment. The photographer called my name for my personal shots. Bianca freshened up my makeup and in moments I was back in front of the flashing lights.

After the photo shoot, Bianca and I headed over to a local café across the street. I stared at my glass of wine while zoning in and out on the conversation Bianca was having with her fiancé. Bianca glanced up to see the vacant expression on my face. She quickly ended the conversation with her beau.

"Rayne, I personally think you are reading way too much into everything," Bianca said as she sipped her wine.

"I just don't know what I am supposed to be feeling. When this whole thing started I was cool. I was actually trying to make him do it when he didn't want to. Now that it's happened I just feel like I have opened a box I can't close."

"Maybe you don't need to close it."

I looked at the serious look on Bianca's face. How could she be okay with what was going on with me?

"Rayne, you are the most dedicated person I know, but you never let go and have a good time. It was sex. This wasn't supposed to be a love affair. It never was. He even told you it wasn't. Stop trying to make this more than what it is. It is just sex."

"With a man, Bianca." I felt my body tensing up. "My whole identity—"

"Your identity is what? God, you gays and your labels." Bianca rolled her eyes. "That's the problem with you people. You can't just let yourself be happy without there being a bloody label attached."

Bianca paused only to allow the waitress to set our plates down. She ordered another glass of wine and waited for the waitress to walk away.

"Rayne, you are not in high school anymore or college. You don't have to label yourself gay or straight. You are just Rayne and you can do whatever the fuck you want because you don't owe shit to anyone or anything."

Bianca's face was turning red. I knew she was serious and only wanted what was best for me. However, watching the angry black girl come out of my white friend was always hilarious to me. I cracked a smile. Bianca shook her head before we both broke out into laughter.

"I swear you got some black in you somewhere."

"I've been around your ass too long." Bianca took another sip of her wine. "You are getting me all upset this afternoon."

I put my hand on my friend's hand. "I hear what you are saying. My brain will catch up I promise."

I knew she was right. I didn't owe anything to anyone. If a man made me happy then who was I to deny myself happiness because it wasn't in the package I expected it to be in? A cool breeze swept over me causing goose bumps to appear on my arms. I felt liberated and free to do whatever I pleased, even if it was Loyal.

Chapter 13

I hadn't been so excited to get to work in a long time. I had accomplished the impossible days before. My artwork was complete and I was ready for the show. I felt like skipping. Bianca kept me busy so that I didn't think about Loyal or the fact that we hadn't spoken in over a week. I'd missed two calls from him during the time but under strict restrictions from Bianca I didn't answer. I expected him to show up at my house like he had done many times before but he never did. It was good. I needed a cleanse from him but Lord knew I missed him.

"Hey, ladies," I said walking over to my bay. I handed white envelopes to Janice and Rosalyn as I had done to the majority of people in our department.

"Oh is this the invitation for next week?" Rosalyn asked as she opened the envelope. "Can I buy the tickets from you?"

"No, they decided just to sell at the venue. You guys are coming?"

"We wouldn't miss it." Janice added, "Loyal, are you going to come too?"

"I still wasn't invited."

I turned around to see Loyal walking toward his desk. My heart skipped a beat. He looked better than I remembered. The white shirt he was wearing seemed to hang on his muscles. I glanced down to see a motorcycle helmet in his hand. My heart started to race. I didn't know he rode motorcycles.

"Oh shit, Loyal, you ride motorcycles?" Janice obviously was impressed too.

"Yeah, didn't I tell you guys that?"

"No, you left that minor detail out." I sat down at my desk. His cologne hit my nostrils alerting all the senses in my body.

"I didn't know you would care."

We made eye contact.

"Is that why that new girl has been hanging around here so much?" Janice took a bite of an apple she had sitting on her desk.

"Ha-ha. No, I doubt it." Loyal looked at me

"New girl?" I turned back around in my chair. Our eyes met again.

"*Sí*." Rosalyn added, "I give it five minutes before she shows up over here. She brings really good snacks though so we allow her to come over."

Janice and Rosalyn both laughed while Loyal nodded his head. He gave me a specific look as to ignore what they were saying, but I knew it was all true.

"Well as long as she's bringing snacks." I laughed it off. I wondered who this new girl was and if this was the reason he hadn't been to my house.

My coworkers were right. Before long a short, thin girl in a skintight black skirt and equally tight shirt sashayed over as though she was walking a runway instead of walking at work. My heart dropped. Unlike the others I'd seen around him this one was very beautiful. Her expensive weave almost looked like it could be real. Her makeup wasn't over done like the majority of the women I saw and even though the clothes were tight, they fit her body like a glove.

"Hello, ladies. Oh you must be Rayne."

Her voice was sensual too. I tried to hold my composure together as she held her hand out to shake my hand.

I simply smiled and turned back to my desk to check e-mails. Through the mirror on my desk I watched her put her hand on Loyal's shoulder before handing him a bag. He thanked her for whatever it was and she mouthed for him to check his e-mail. She walked away and Rosalyn and Janice immediately started rummaging through the bag of goodies she brought for Loyal.

My whole body was numb. I couldn't see straight or think. I couldn't compete with her; it was impossible and I knew it. Of course he would like her, even I would fuck her. I wanted to cry. Everything was making sense. This was why he hadn't been to my house. He had a beautiful new body to snuggle up to. I felt my hand pulling on my shirt. Suddenly I didn't feel comfortable in my clothes. I just wanted to go home but the day had just begun.

"Where's my invitation?"

I felt Loyal's hand touch my shoulder causing me to almost jump out of my skin. I turned, looking down at the floor. I couldn't look at him in his face. I was afraid of what might happen if I did. I handed him a white envelope and turned back to my desk.

"Rayne?"

"I'm kinda busy." My voice cracked. I popped my eyes open as far as they could go. I didn't want tears to fall. I didn't want to look weak. Loyal didn't press me. He continued to laugh with Janice and Rosalyn, leaving me to check my e-mail.

The hours went by fast. We found ourselves left alone once the final coworker left our bay. I could feel the anxiety starting to grow. I knew we were going to have to talk at some point; I just didn't want the time to come so fast.

"Hey."

The familiar voice instantly irritated me. I turned to see the same girl walking back over to our section.

"What's up?" Loyal responded in his usual calm tone. The girl pulled Janice's chair out and sat in it. There was no hesitation. It was obvious this was something she had done before. I tried to remain calm, focusing on my sketchpad while they talked about random things from work to working out. The girl asked him if he was going to the gym that night. Loyal calmly said he wasn't sure.

"So you are an artist right?"

I realized that the girl was talking to me. I turned around to see her smiling at me. "Yes."

"That's so cool. Loyal was telling me that you were having a show soon."

My eyes met Loyal's. I could tell he knew I was upset. He stayed calm, just wearing a straight-faced expression.

"I love art. I might have to check that out." She stood up. "Well it was nice meeting you. Day, I'll talk to you later." She touched him on his shoulder before walking away.

I spun back around toward my computer screen. I felt the room closing in on me. My heart was racing.

"Rayne."

Before I could stop myself I whipped my chair back around. "Well at least you were nice enough to tell your new bitch about me. Nice."

Loyal shook his head. He didn't seem fazed by my anger at all.

"So is this the new look? I go away for a few days and you got another chick already making herself comfortable."

"Rayne—"

"Whatever, Loyal. Or should I say Day. Ugh." I turned back to my desk.

Loyal didn't respond. He shook his head and stared back at his computer screen.

This calmness angered me even more. Not only did he hurt me by having his new woman around but he didn't seem to care at all that I was upset. I wanted to hit him but I knew I was at work. I couldn't wait for the final hour to be up.

We continued to ignore each other for the rest of the night. I could hear him typing on his keyboard. I knew he wasn't doing work. I figured he was e-mailing his new boo. Every now and then I would hear his phone go off. It was probably one of the other women he was romancing while taking his break from me.

The end of the day finally came. I knew we were going to have it out, probably in the parking lot or sitting in my car. I began packing my bag up. Before I could finish I watched Loyal grab his paperwork and helmet, and walk out the door.

I was mortified.

I grabbed my bags as quickly as I could and headed out the door. Outside I saw Loyal putting his helmet on. His bike was a beautiful turquoise blue and black, which only made him look sexier. I quickly walked over to him before he could take off.

"So you just gon' walk off like that?"

"Got things to do."

"So we aren't going to talk?"

Loyal looked at me with a serious face. "Not now. Later. But not now."

I watched him put his helmet on and take off leaving me standing in the dark parking lot by myself.

I wanted to cry.

I felt my world crashing down around me. I didn't deserve the treatment he was giving me. After all he was in the wrong. It was only normal to not want to be in the presence of his other women. Why would he think that was okay?

My phone began to ring. I fumbled through my bag until finally finding it. My heart dropped when it wasn't Loyal. Instead Pashun's name appeared on the screen. I rolled my eyes and answered the phone.

"Good evening, Rayne. I hope I'm not interrupting you."

I rolled my eyes as I started walking to my car. "No, what's up, Pashun?"

"I actually have something for you. I was wondering if I could bring it by."

I paused. I pulled my keys out and got in my car. Loyal had already ruined my night; maybe a little company could take my mind off of him. "I'll be home in about fifteen minutes."

I pulled up to my building to see Pashun sitting outside. He had a large canvas sitting next to him. He stood up as I walked up to the door. His jeans were baggy but didn't actually fall off his body and his white button-down shirt clung to his body showing off how slender he truly was. "Hey."

I forced a smile the best I could as I walked toward him. He stretched his long arms out and gave me a hug. We walked up my walkway and into my house.

Pashun followed me to the living room. I offered him a seat and asked if he wanted something to drink. He asked for some water. I turned and headed to the kitchen, a little upset that he actually asked for something back. This meant he wouldn't just be dropping off whatever it was to me. I made it back in the living room to find him staring at one of my paintings on the wall.

"You've taken some different directions with your work I see." Pashun was standing in front of the same portrait that Loyal examined his first time at my house. His long, slender fingers were stroking his beard.

"Just trying some new stuff." I walked over.

Pashun turned around with a very sullen expression on his face. "I see."

He took the water from my hands. He stared at me as he took a sip of the cold water. I suddenly felt uneasy. I took a few steps back.

"So you said you had something for me?"

Pashun's expression changed drastically. His tight lips curled up giving him a cute grin exposing the deep right dimple in his cheek. He walked over and picked up the canvas he brought with him. He walked back over to me holding the canvas so I couldn't see what was on it.

"So the other day when we did the photo shoot I noticed your expression a few times. I couldn't quite put my finger on it but I couldn't get it out of my mind. So . . ."

He turned the canvas around and my mouth dropped.

"I painted it."

I stared at the image on the canvas. It felt surreal; he had captured me as well as any camera could by just using various shades of blue and black.

"Oh my God, Pashun, wow." My fingers traced the outline of my painted lips. "I guess I don't really smile much do I?" I looked up to see Pashun's face locked on me.

He smiled. "No, you aren't big on smiling. That's normal. It was your eyes that caught my attention."

I glanced at Pashun who motioned for me to look back at the canvas. I stared at the eyes. An unsettled feeling came over me. "They look so . . . I'm not sure."

"Yeah, I know. You know as long as I've known you, Rayne, you have been a determined chick. You have always been nice but you could tell that nothing else mattered but you succeeding. Yet at the photo shoot, where you are standing on the brink of the success you desire, there wasn't happiness or any type of fulfillment in your eyes. Na, mama, you just looked lost."

Lost? I repeated the word in my head over and over. An ache hit me in the pit of my stomach. I didn't want him looking at me. I turned away and stared at my own painting on the wall. I could feel Pashun as he walked closer to me until standing directly behind me.

"When I saw this picture it just solidified it for me. I don't know what might be going on, and I'm not going to pry. But just know that, whatever it is, you don't have to go through it alone. You have a friend in me, Rayne, a friend who is ready to see some joy back in your eyes."

I turned around to find myself looking directly at Pashun's chest. His tall frame towered over me. He put his right index finger on my chin, pushing my face upward until our eyes met. My heart was beating faster than normal, and a slight tingling was overcoming my body. But it wasn't the same. It wasn't as electric as I knew it could be.

"I wanna show you something." I pulled away before the moment got the best of both of us.

We headed down my hallway until three faint knocks at my door caused us both to pause. I felt my body tighten up, unable to move from the spot I was in.

"You expecting someone?" Pashun asked as he looked at the door.

"Um . . ." I knew who it was. There was only one person who knocked like that. I panicked. I couldn't think of what I was supposed to do in that situation. How could I explain another man being in my house? My mind raced with alternative options. I could have Pashun wait in my studio while I got rid of Loyal, but I didn't want to get rid of Loyal.

"I can get the door if you like." Pashun looked at me.

The girl from earlier popped into my head. Suddenly things seemed clear. Why was I getting worked up over Pashun being at my house when Loyal flaunted his new conquest in front of me at work?

"You know what, that's great. You can grab the door while I get things ready in here. It's probably just Bianca or a neighbor."

I walked into my art room. I stood on the side of the door and listened as Pashun opened the door. I couldn't hear what was being said but in moments I heard two sets of footsteps headed in my direction. I rushed over to my paint area and picked up an apron like I was really about to do some work.

"Sup, Rayne."

I turned around holding the apron in my hand. Loyal and Pashun both stood at the entrance of my art studio. Loyal had his usual smirk on his face while Pashun's face let me know he was curious about this man in my house.

"Loyal, I didn't know you were coming by." I forced my legs to move closer to the two men.

"Yeah, I was in the area and just thought I would drop by, see how you are doing."

"Oh I'm good." I held my arms out. "Oh, Loyal, this is Pashun. Pashun, this is Loyal."

The two men shook hands. They were so different but so much alike at the same time. Both had their own special swag about them. While Loyal oozed sex appeal in a more masculine way, Pashun's sexiness came from his amazing features and artistic abilities.

"Well I'm going to get out of your hair. I was just dropping by. I will see you at work." Loyal winked at me before walking to the door.

Pashun followed Loyal to the door just as though he was the man of the house for real. I exhaled, happy that I made it through the moment without losing all cool. Moments later Pashun appeared back in the door. "So, coworker?"

"Yeah."

Pashun nodded his head as he walked farther into the room. "So what are you going to show me?"

One by one I unveiled all the portraits I was showing in the show. Pashun gave me his honest opinion on each. It was refreshing to hear his thoughts. I agreed with him on many of his opinions and even made a mental note to change a few of the things he mentioned on a few of the paintings.

"Okay so show me the big guy."

"What?" I smiled.

Pashun walked over to the sculpture that was obviously draped under the large white sheet. "I know you didn't think you were going to show me all these paintings and not show me the sculpture."

I felt nervous. No one had seen the sculpture besides Loyal. I suddenly didn't want anyone to see it, ever.

"Should I move the sheet or you?" Pashun smiled.

"Fine." I took a deep breath and removed the sheet from the sculpture. Pashun froze. A few seconds later he took three steps back. I watched as his eyes squinted. He walked around, studying the art piece from all sides.

"Well?" The anticipation was killing me.

Pashun stared at me without saying anything. I could feel him trying to see inside of me. Uneasy, I turned toward the sculpture so that he couldn't see my face.

"Are you going to answer me?" I could hear the rise in octave in my voice. The man was making me nervous.

Pashun walked back over next to me. He looked at the sculpture then looked at me. "It's good, Rayne. It's really, really good."

Shocked, I turned to see him nodding his head with a slight smile on his face. "You really think so?"

"Yes. The lines are amazing. The color jumps out. I personally would add a little more gloss on a few areas just to help them pop a little more but overall it's amazing. Super sexy but haunting at the same time."

"Haunting?" The use of word caught me off-guard.

Pashun nodded his head. "Yeah, I mean look at the way the hands are holding the woman. It's not endearing or romantic; it's hard, abrasive. This isn't a loving embrace by any means."

His words hit me like a ton of bricks. "I wouldn't say that." I stuttered a bit.

"Oh, Rayne, come on you have to see it. It's obvious there isn't love in this, it's just sex. Look at how he's gripping her body. That's not the way a man who loves a woman would hold her. But then again I guess you wouldn't really know that."

My head snapped around toward Pashun who was still focused on the sculpture unaware that he had just offended me. "You don't know what you are talking about, Pashun. I know what I am talking about. I designed the thing. There is passion and more in that embrace."

"Yeah, no, sorry, not buying it." Pashun shook his head.

"And how the hell would you know what I know about? I've been held before, asshole. What you think I don't have sex or something?" I was heated.

Pashun's glanced at me completely confused by my outburst. "Rayne, I'm sure you have sex, but this sculpture screams that you don't know shit about being with a man. It's just like you lesbians to make sex with a man seem so hard."

I froze again. I completely forgot that Pashun, like most people, thought that I was a lesbian. His thoughts would have made perfect sense if this was done pre-Loyal. Loyal's face appeared in my mind. Was Pashun right? I had been with a man and this was what I sculpted from the experience. Was I wrong in my design, or were there really no true feelings involved in the experience?

"Show me."

Pashun's face quickly turned to me. I stared at him. I had to know if there was a difference.

"Show you what?" Pashun's hands dropped to his side. "You say that isn't endearing. What is endearing? Show me."

"Um, are you for real?"

"Very."

Pashun hesitated for a brief moment. I could tell by the look on Pashun's face that he was taken aback by my request, but like any man staring at something he's wanted for a long time he wasn't about to let the moment pass. He slowly walked closer to me. He stood behind me, so close I could feel his manhood pressing against my ass.

"When a man cares about a woman he doesn't hold her the same way he holds the bitches he might fuck with on the side."

I felt his soft slender hands touching my sides. I closed my eyes.

"He knows that she is gentle and should be treated as such. Not gentle in a way that she might break if held too hard, but gentle in the way of knowing that prized possessions should be handled with care."

His hands moved from my sides until reaching all the way around me. His body pressed firmly against my backside.

"But what if the woman wants to be held rough?" I asked.

"Oh he can do that, too. But there's still a difference."

I felt a familiar surge of energy as Pashun's arms quickly pulled me in as close as I could be. It was forceful, but not rough.

"When you care about something, you don't want to see it in pain; you only want it to feel happiness and pleasure."

Pashun ran his fingers from the top of my head. I could feel his energy as he softly grazed my scalp until pushing my hair over my right shoulder.

"You don't do things that could hurt the thing. You make it your mission not to."

Pashun's fingers grazed the nape of my neck sending chills down my spine. I felt my panties becoming moist from his touch.

I pulled away.

I turned to see Pashun standing with an odd smirk on his face. He shook his head. "Do you see the difference?"

"Maybe." I flashed a devilish grin back. I could tell he was intrigued. He had never come so close to me before. I could almost hear his mind working overtime trying to decide to make a move or not.

"*A Lover's Embrace.*"

"What?" I responded.

"Call the piece *A Lover's Embrace*. But with a question mark on the end. I gotta run. It's been real, Rayne. We should do this more often."

Pashun hugged me tight. I could feel the erection in his pants. I knew he didn't want to leave but I applauded him for not trying to make another move on me. He kissed my hand before I let him out the front door. I headed back to my kitchen but something caught my eye. I picked up the portrait he did of me. Sitting next to it my cell phone notification light was blinking. I turned it on to see a missed text message from ten minutes earlier.

LOYAL: Still got company?

I held my phone for a moment contemplating my response. There was a distinct difference in what Pashun did versus Loyal. It was no secret that Loyal wasn't in love with me or even close. I wasn't his girl. But could he actually sleep with me and not have any feelings for me whatsoever? I wanted to know. I needed to know the truth.

RAYNE: No. The door is open.

Chapter 14

I heard his footsteps as he walked into my house. I lay in my bed wearing nothing but a short silk kimono-style robe Bianca had given me a few years earlier that I never had a reason to wear. Loyal walked in my bedroom and smiled.

"Did you have fun tonight?" he asked as he took his shoes off and laid his jacket on a chair.

"It was nice. He gave me some insight on my art."

"Insight huh?" Loyal asked as he crawled on top of the bed next to me.

"Yes." I turned around toward Loyal. He began to unbutton his pants. He pushed them off. Something different for the man who always laid things out perfectly so he wouldn't look wrinkled when he left my house.

"About Kelis."

Skinny bitch had a name after all.

"I don't care." I frowned.

"Yes, you do. And yes, she is someone who is trying to get with me. But I won't fuck her."

"Yeah, right."

Loyal shook his head. "You see the way she is at my desk. That is signs of trouble to come. I would never fuck with a girl who is that obvious with what we do at work. You would never know the women I mess with up at the job because they are never around me at work."

I sat up. "Wait a minute. Just how many women are you fucking with at our job?"

Loyal's lip curled.

"I'm serious. Tell me."

"You mean right now? Probably four."

"What!" I tried to get out of the bed but he grabbed my arms.

"Rayne, don't start. You know the business."

"I didn't know that meant I was one in a harem of woman at our fucking company. Fuck, are any of them in our department?"

"Maybe. Maybe not."

"Ugh." I pulled away from him and got out of the bed. I began to pace the floor. Pashun was right; there was no way in the world this man actually cared about what we were doing.

"So what the fuck, Loyal? What am I to you? Am I just another bitch you are fucking? Was I the 'turn a lesbian out' notch on your belt?"

Loyal sat up in my bed. He wouldn't take his eyes off of me. The facial expression was daunting. I couldn't read him. I had no idea what he was thinking and it was driving me completely up the wall.

He continued to stare at me in silence. I wanted to know what he was thinking. Was he coming up with an elaborate lie to appease me and my out-of-control feelings? Maybe he was trying to come up with the right way to tell me that he wasn't going to deal with me or my mouth.

"Why are you here, Loyal? You obviously have others. Why are you here? What am I to you?"

Loyal shook his head. "Rayne, I told you this shit was going to happen," Loyal said as he got out of my bed.

"Loyal, I have not changed. I am still the same person. I don't need you to be my man, but I need to know what the fuck am I? Is this some casual-ass shit that doesn't mean anything at all?"

Loyal walked up to me. His cologne was making me weak in the knees. "Rayne, if you were some random piece you think I would stay over like I do? Do you think I get comfortable at some random bitch's house? I spend time with you. I sleep with you. So what are you to me? My friend, or at least that's what I thought."

I felt my jaw twinge. One side of me felt terrible that I was acting like a jealous girlfriend, while the other side felt I was being fed a load of garbage. The worst part was that each side was equal, so I had no idea which to believe in.

"Rayne, you are my friend. I don't say that too often especially to women but I think we are more. I told you that fucking you would do this."

I watched Loyal pick up his things. My heart dropped. I might have been upset but the one thing I didn't want was for him to leave me.

"Loyal, I just wanted clarity. We are cool." I grabbed his hand. I didn't want him to leave me that night. It was as if gravity was pulling me closer to him. A part of me knew it was best to let him go, but a bigger part knew I couldn't let him walk out.

The bigger part won.

Chapter 15

Things weren't getting better at work but I couldn't focus on it. Not only did the girl feel the need to come over on all her breaks but she was becoming cool with my other coworkers. Even if Loyal wasn't around or was stuck on a phone call she had other people to talk to besides him. I maintained my distance by always focusing on my work or drawing in my pad whenever she came over.

Loyal told me he wouldn't sleep with a woman who acted like her, but I couldn't shake the feeling that he had slept with her. I'd seen my other coworkers who were dating people in different departments and it was the same as she was. They spent time at each other's desks, brought snacks and little presents. She wasn't missing a beat. Every day there was some new treat that she found at Whole Foods that she knew would cater to his love of healthy foods.

"Hey, Rayne, so your show is right around the corner isn't it?"

I truly hated that she felt so comfortable talking to me. "Yeah, three days."

Kelis smiled. "That is so awesome. I really am going to try to make it," she said as she spun the chair from side to side.

I faked a smile before turning back to my drawing.

"So have you decided to go yet, Lo?"

I cringed. Not only did I hate the idea of her attempting to bring Loyal to my opening as her date, but the fact that she used nicknames on him irritated me to no end.

"I don't know. I'll probably roll through for a second. I think I have something else to do that night."

I smiled. Loyal knew I would kill him if he showed up with her.

"Well you should let me know. I can get us tickets." Kelis playfully hit Loyal on his knee.

Kelis stood up and pushed the chair back under the desk. She said her good-bye before her usual sashay back to her own department. I rolled my eyes causing Loyal to laugh.

"I really wish you would tell your little girlfriend to stay the fuck away from this bay." I rolled my neck with attitude.

"That's so messed up. This girl is nice to you and even trying to come to your exhibit but you wanna call her names." Loyal smiled.

"She can come to the exhibit all she wants. By herself."

Loyal laughed. He shrugged his shoulders. "I don't know, she is offering to pay for me."

"Loyal, don't play with me." I stared at him. He didn't flinch. I had no idea if he was playing.

"Well I'm just saying this girl has offered to take me out to dinner and pay for the evening. I don't know if I can pass that up."

I wanted to think he was playing but the look on his face led me to believe that it was a distinct possibility that he would take her up on her offer.

"I will leave a ticket at will call in your name. Now you have no reason to come with anyone because your ticket is already taken care of," I folded my arms and huffed.

"Aw isn't that sweet of you." Loyal winked at me and smiled. I shook my head. He was charming and I hated it almost as much as I loved it.

***

I put my book bag on my shoulder and grabbed my car keys. "Am I seeing you tonight?"

I watched Loyal type away on his phone. He finally acknowledged me by looking up. "Um, probably, I'll call."

He walked out ahead of me. I followed as I headed out of the call center. Loyal looked back to see me walking behind him. Something seemed off; was he trying to lose me?

"Bye, Rayne." He waved as he headed into the men's bathroom right by the back door. I had a sneaking suspicion he was up to something. A large piece of me wanted to wait by the door and see when he was going to come out. I knew there would be no way for me to explain that so I shook it off and headed to my car.

I started my car and turned on my iPod. I noticed Loyal's car in the distance. I wanted to wait, sit back with my lights off, and watch when he came out. My hand almost turned my engine off when I saw the door open. Standing there was Kelis, and right behind her Loyal walked out. She walked with him to her car. I watched her hand him something before he gave her a hug. She sat in her car while he rested his hand on her door. I watched how relaxed he was with her. He was flashing his golden smile and she was eating up every moment of it.

My phone rang pulling me out of the train wreck I knew I was about to witness. I drove off before answering the phone.

"Hello?" I answered without paying attention to the caller ID.

"Uh-oh, what's wrong with you?" Kevin asked.

I took a deep breath. "Oh nothing just got a lot on my mind." I couldn't stop thinking about what was happening back at our parking lot. How far did things go between them? Did I witness all that would happen or would Loyal take it further?

"I figured as much. Just wanted to check in and make sure you weren't about to hurl yourself off of a bridge."

I smiled. Kevin had a way of making me smile when no one else could. "Kevin."

"Sup, hon?"

"If you knew a girl cared about you but you have already told her that you aren't going to be her boyfriend, would you continue to sleep with her even though you know you will never want her?"

Kevin paused. I knew he was trying to analyze the question. He knew that I would only ask something like that if there was a reason behind it.

"Well, me personally, no. I've outgrown the days of leading women on."

"Yeah, but what if you aren't leading them on? What if you have told them that there would never be a relationship and she says she's okay with it?"

I watched Kevin's head shaking back and forth as I pleaded my point.

"Actions speak ten times louder than words, Rayne. I don't care if the girl swears up and down that it is just casual; if her actions are showing otherwise I'm going to break it off. In the end, as a grown man, I don't want to see any woman hurt because of me."

I let his words sink in. "Okay, I hear you, but what if it's the other way around? What if you are feeling a girl who says she doesn't want a relationship, but she does things that lead you to believe that maybe she cares more than she leads on?"

I heard Kevin chuckle a little bit. "Rayne, in the end none of that stuff matters. If a person tells me that they don't want a relationship with me then I am ending it if I know that is what I want. Why would I invest my time, money, and energy into someone who isn't looking for what I am looking for?"

"Yeah, but things can change," I added.

"They can, but why take that chance when you can go out there and find someone who does want what you want? That's the problem; so many people get involved in relationships when they are already on two different floors. So you spend the whole relationship trying to play catch-up."

"Okay, I hear ya." I smiled.

"Now who are you involved with who doesn't want a relationship?" Kevin's voice got deeper with the question. I knew he was concerned when I heard the lower octave.

I wanted to tell him what was happening but I didn't want him to worry about me. I was tired of my friends worrying about me when it came to love and relationships. "It's nothing like that. I met someone but they said they aren't trying to get into a relationship and don't want one anytime soon. I was just trying to figure out if I should still consider taking them up on their offer for a date."

There was a long pause. I looked at the phone to make sure the call didn't drop in a bad spot.

"Rayne, never ever date someone you like more than they like you. A person should be one hundred and ten percent about you. If they aren't, they don't deserve you."

I could hear someone knocking on Kevin's door.

"Gotta run, sweetie; we will pick this up later."

"Okay."

"Wait, Rayne," Kevin yelled hoping I hadn't hung up.

"Yeah?"

"Just remember what I said. Know your worth, babes, 'cause you are worth millions."

Kevin's words warmed my heart.

I made it home with a new sense of purpose. I wasn't going to wait on Loyal. Even if he called I wasn't going to allow him to come over. I poured myself a glass of wine and decided to catch up on shows. Just as I expected my DVR was filled with episodes of shows I had missed.

Three hours, three shows, and a bottle of wine later there was still no call and I felt horrible. I decided to turn in instead of letting my mind run away with all types of thoughts. I curled up in my bed. A familiar scent filled my nose. I smelled the pillow Loyal usually slept on. His cologne covered the pillow.

I wanted to cry. I put myself in an impossible situation. I wanted this man more than I had ever wanted anyone before, yet he didn't want me back. I broke the rules. I had fallen for him and I had fallen hard.

As I held on to his pillow I knew it wasn't sex I wanted. I didn't care about the sex. I never cared about sex. I wanted him. I wanted to feel his body next to mine. It was him, from the way he wrapped his arms around me to the way he said my name. I wanted to laugh with him and listen to him tell me that my art was amazing. Nothing else mattered.

Finally the Sandman found me. I fell asleep gripping the pillow he slept on, now covered in my tears.

Chapter 16

"Stop that!" Bianca hit my hand.

She had already told me a million times to stop pulling at the dress I had on but I couldn't help it. I knew she had picked out an amazing dress for me. The elegant maxi dress was form-fitting at the top, gripping my breasts just right, but the bottomed flowed freely. The black dress had splashes of color as though I had taken my paintbrush and painted beautiful lines all over it. It was perfect for the occasion, but I still couldn't help but think that everyone would be paying attention to the rolls of fat I felt were showing. I looked at myself in the mirror again. Thanks to the miracle Spanx I was as smooth as I could possibly be.

"You look fabulous," Bianca gushed.

"You think?" I raised my hand to rub my eye.

Bianca hit my hand. "Don't you fucking dare. I will kill you if you mess up your makeup."

From the evil eye Bianca gave me I knew she was serious.

"Ladies, the car is outside."

We turned to see Bianca's fiancé standing in the door. I smiled. I was happy my friend found someone perfect for her. Matthew looked like he stepped off of the cover of *GQ*. He had the features of many of the white men I had on my hottie list. His chiseled jaw line and gray eyes were stunning. I joked that together they looked like they belonged on the cover of a book or advertising some perfume collection.

We got in the Town Car and headed to the event. I could feel my nerves attempting to get the best of me as we arrived. Bianca rubbed my hand telling me to relax. I took deep breaths to calm my nerves. I almost took Bianca up on taking one of her many pills but knew that would be a bad idea in the long run. I didn't need to fall asleep while trying to show off my work.

As we arrived I saw a few of my coworkers standing in line to get tickets. I smiled; they were actually there to support me. I had taken the last two days off. I didn't want to be around Loyal or Kelis for fear of what I might say or do.

I hadn't heard from Loyal since my last day at work. He didn't call and I didn't either. After filling Bianca in with the whole situation between Loyal and me she said what I knew I needed to do. I needed to distance myself so I could get my feelings in check. I consumed myself with trying to relax. I watched TV, played video games, and spent time allowing Bianca to take me shopping for things for her wedding. The good thing was the distractions seemed to be working. Thoughts of Loyal only consumed me at night, before I went to bed, still sleeping with his pillow in my arms.

I felt my hands tensing up. I wondered if he was already inside. I'd left his ticket at will call and wanted to ask as I walked in but knew Bianca would kill me if she knew that I'd given him a ticket to the show.

I arrived inside to claps from my coworkers, associates, and family who had shown up for the event. I walked over to my portion of the show to find people already crowded around my sculpture. I noticed Pashun standing with a much larger crowd, but that was to be expected.

As the night started I greeted the other artists and the movers and shakers who were in the building. In between explaining my various pieces to people I chatted with my guests and others. An hour passed and Loyal was still nowhere to be found. I forced myself to remain calm. I knew I couldn't focus on it. I figured he was just going to make a late appearance.

Two hours passed and it was time to start the official presentation. The crowds walked around to each artist's section. We listened as the artist gave their presentations. I found myself looking back at the door over and over. I was going to kill him if he missed my presentation.

Pashun's large-scale painting caught the eyes of everyone. I couldn't help but admire how he commanded the crowd with his words. He was born to do this.

"I think your only competition is Pashun. That son of a bitch is rather brilliant." Bianca walked up and handed me a glass of champagne. "Why do you keep looking at the door?"

"I . . ."

"You are waiting on that boy aren't you? Well rest assured, he's here."

I turned to see Loyal walking in the door.

Behind him Kelis walked in.

My heart dropped out of my chest.

"I am going to kick his ass." Bianca started to walk but I grabbed her arm.

"No, let it be. I have to get ready for my presentation and, I need you here."

I held my best friend's hand as we walked back over to my section. The crowd made its way over with me. I wanted to cry but I knew it wasn't the time for it. I threw back the glass of champagne and put on the biggest smile I could muster.

"You got this, Rayne. Fuck him and the two-bit ghetto slut he walked in with. You are better than them. This is your night. No one can take that from you. Now go do your thing."

I hugged Bianca and took a deep breath. The crowd completely formed around my section. I saw Pashun standing in the back. He gave me a thumbs-up, which made me feel a little better. I tried not to but my eyes focused back on Loyal who was standing with our other coworkers. He looked at me with a smile on his face. How could he smile when he knew what he did was going to crush me?

"Ladies and gentlemen, I want to thank you all for allowing me to showcase my talent for you tonight. As far as my theme, there really isn't a theme. I started out with a theme in my head but in the end I honestly just let my emotions take control."

One by one I explained each painting. I watched as people's heads nodded at the ones they enjoyed most. I made my way around the five until ending with my sculpture.

"With the help of a friend I named this piece *A Lover's Embrace?* When I started sculpting it I believed that there was true passion in the hands. I felt that there was a real connection. As I finished I realized that . . ."

I looked over at Loyal who was staring at me. I felt the ball of emotions that I swallowed trying to force its way out. I took a deep breath.

"I realized that you can believe in something or someone but that doesn't mean they have to feel the same way. People say that actions speak louder than words. Well with this piece I show that actions can read differently to different people. So is it or isn't it a loving embrace? You decide."

Tears flowed as the crowd clapped for me. I smiled hoping that the tears read as tears of joy and not of a woman whose heart was breaking right in front of them. Pashun walked up and wrapped his long arms around me.

"That was fucking amazing, love." Pashun kissed me on my cheek.

I knew the night was just beginning. I was surrounded by people praising my talent. I saw Bianca to the side busy with potential buyers. Pashun was back over in his own section, no doubt selling all of his pieces if they weren't already sold.

I hoped I could stay away from them. As long as people surrounded me or I looked like I was engaged in important conversation I knew he wouldn't come over. My plan went out the window as they opened the buffet. The crowd died down as people filled their plates with finger foods. I looked away for a moment to catch my breath only to turn around to find Kelis and Loyal standing in front of me.

Kelis wrapped her arms around me. "You were amazing, Rayne. I am so excited for you."

"You really were amazing, Raynedrop." Loyal put his hand on my arm.

I didn't know what to say. I wanted to curse him out but remembered my surroundings. He knew I wouldn't cause a scene because of where we were. I was speechless. I felt like the walls were closing in on me.

"How much for them all?"

I heard a voice whisper behind me. I turned around and almost jumped out of my body. Kevin stood behind me with a large smile on his face. He looked amazing with his various medals from the Air Force adorning his jacket.

"Oh my God." I threw my arms around my friend. He laughed as he held me tight. All the emotions I felt came flooding out. I held on to him unable to let go.

"I guess you missed me huh?" Kevin laughed as he continued to hold me.

Realizing I wasn't letting go, Kevin finally pulled me back. My face was covered in tears. He used his hand to wipe the tears from my face. "It's okay, doll, stop crying."

"I just can't believe you are here." I sobbed like a little girl.

I didn't realize how much I missed my friend. I turned around to see Loyal and Kelis standing there with Bianca and a few others who all witnessed the reunion. I saw tears in Bianca's eyes, which was different because she never cried.

Loyal looked at me with an inquisitive look. I realized he had no idea who the guy was who just gave me the biggest shock of my life. I decided to use it to my advantage. I put my arm around Kevin. He held on to me as he greeted Bianca and Matthew. I no longer acknowledged Loyal's existence. It was all about Kevin and he soaked up the spotlight. No one could resist a beautiful man in uniform.

I never had so many emotions going on in one night. I wanted to be happy that Kevin flew in just for the night, and I really wanted to celebrate the fact that my sculpture had a bidding war going between two different people. I continued to float around the building, smiling and socializing while my eyes shifted until they met Loyal's face. Kelis never seemed to leave his side. They looked like the perfect couple, and made a lot more sense than Loyal and I ever did. The realization was settling in: Loyal would never be mine.

The other piece of me was furious. Loyal wasn't dumb by any means so he knew that showing up to my gallery opening with another woman would hurt me. However, he took it a step further and not only showed up with another woman, but with the one he already knew I had a sensitive spot about. I couldn't hide behind any smoke and mirrors. He had slapped me with the truth and I couldn't hide from it even if I wanted to. The undeniable truth was Loyal just didn't give a damn about me at the end of the day.

I didn't care about the exhibit anymore. I wanted to get out of the building before I had a complete breakdown. I needed some fresh air. I dipped out the side door hoping that no one saw me. The crisp air alerted my senses. I took a deep breath only to get a strong whiff of cigarette smoke.

"Needed a break too huh?"

I turned around to see Pashun's tall frame appear from the side. Pashun walked closer, dropping his lit cigarette on the ground before pressing his foot on it to extinguish it.

"Yeah, a break."

"Yeah." Pashun nodded his head. "I can dig it. These things can be a bit hard to handle." He paused for a moment while I stared at the lights on the tall buildings in the distance.

"Especially when the person you care about shows up with someone else."

My body froze. I turned my face toward Pashun to see the serious look on his face.

"Was I that obvious?" I could feel my hands starting to tense up again. If Pashun noticed I knew in my mind that others had to notice as well.

Pashun shook his head. "Na, you weren't that obvious. I am just very attentive at times. I could tell you were upset. I really wanted to fuck ol' boy up."

I couldn't help but smile. Pashun put his hand on my right cheek. The simple touch warmed my soul. "Don't let some nigga ruin your night. Trust me he will be back. How could anyone stay away from you? Let's get back in before they call your name as winner and you aren't there."

"Whatever." I laughed as I followed Pashun back into the building.

I walked back in with a boost of confidence. The crowd was gathering around the stage. My eyes instantly went to Loyal who was finally standing without his date. Bianca grabbed my arm as it was time for the winners to be announced. She quickly freshened up my makeup before I walked on stage with the other artists. I stood next to Pashun who put his arm around me. I couldn't help but notice the smirk on Loyal's face.

The director of the gallery came on stage with the mayor and a few other high-profile people in the art community of Memphis. They made speeches about how amazing we all were and about how we should preserve the arts in the city. I found myself wishing I'd opted for flats as my feet were killing me.

Finally it was time for them to announce the awards. Suddenly nothing else mattered. I didn't care about Loyal who was now back with his date. I knew I didn't need to look in his direction. I glanced over at Kevin who was standing with Bianca. He gave me a thumbs-up. I smiled, took a deep breath, and waited for the name to be called.

Pashun won.

I hugged him as the cameras flashed and people cheered. I watched as my friend accepted his award. He thanked everyone and even mentioned how he felt like we were all winners. I was disappointed, but not nearly as upset as I thought I would have been. I couldn't be upset about anything else that night; my mind wouldn't allow me to be.

Kevin wrapped his arms around me when I came off of the stage. "I'm sorry, boo." His baritone voice provided a comfort that was welcomed.

"It's cool. I think we all knew who was going to take the prize." I smiled. It was one of the first times I didn't feel the need to actually force the smile on my face.

Camille punched away on her phone. "Well here is something to be very excited for." She held her phone up.

Kevin's mouth and mine dropped open at the same time. My paintings and sculpture sold for close to $12,000. I hugged my best friends. Suddenly Loyal didn't matter. I had better things to think about.

Chapter 17

Kevin wouldn't take his eyes off of me. We sat on my bed eating popcorn and drinking wine while I informed him on the whole Loyal fiasco. He didn't move; he just listened as I poured all my feelings out with the bottle of wine I had already consumed.

Even hearing myself talk about it was surreal. I had allowed myself to fall for a guy who made it perfectly clear that I would never be more than a friend he fucked. I bamboozled myself into believing I could be intimate with someone without having actual feelings for him. I felt incredibly stupid.

"Stop it."

I looked up to see Kevin still staring at me.

"Rayne, will you stop internalizing this situation?" Kevin poured some more wine in my glass.

"What do you mean?" I asked as I sipped.

"Sweetie, you sleeping with this man was not the reason that you are in the situation you are in now. You didn't fall for him over sex; hell you don't even like sex like that."

"I liked it with him," I confessed.

Kevin frowned. "I'm sure you enjoyed whatever you guys did but that is because you are an adult and sex is great. But the reason you are hurting is because you let him in on a intellectual level, not sexual."

We sat in silence while I pondered the thought. Loyal was the first guy I allowed into my art space since Kevin.

"I did feel a connection before the sex." I nodded my head.

"That's because you fall for people because of their personalities not because of what they can do to you sexually. Even with your ex-girlfriends, the ones you were most in love with were the ones you had a friendship with first."

Kevin got off the bed. He put the wine bottle on my dresser. "Rayne, this dude isn't your friend. He's a coworker you occasionally screw. You need to treat him as such."

"But he is the one who said that he values my friendship."

"He doesn't value shit, Rayne. If he did he never would have shown up tonight with the other chick. You don't do that for someone you care about. You don't purposely hurt them. Tonight he acted like a coworker you occasionally fuck, not as a friend. So from now on treat him the same way."

I stared at my best friend. Kevin had been there for me since we were in elementary school. We never crossed the line even after all the years of being friends. He stood in my mirror brushing his hair wearing a simple white T-shirt and a pair of designer lounge pants that seemed to hang on his body just right. I'd never looked at him in a sexual way before.

"Kevin, why have you never tried anything with me? Let's face it; there's been plenty of drunken nights that you probably could have."

Kevin turned around with a frown on his face. "Why would I want your drunk pussy?" He shook his head.

"You know what I mean." I threw a pillow at him, which he caught with one hand. "You haven't said anything about how it feels to know all of this is happening and it's with a man."

Kevin sighed as he sat back on the bed. "I mean it's strange to hear my lesbian friend has been turned out by some Hispanic Rico Suave but hey things happen. I always figured you would want to come back to the light one of these days; you could have picked a brotha."

We both laughed. Kevin sat back resting against my headboard. I moved closer laying my head on his legs. I closed my eyes as he ran his fingers through my hair.

"I've created a mess of a life haven't I?" I sighed.

"Na, you actually are doing pretty amazing. You just need to see what we see and it will be all good."

I fell asleep in Kevin's arms. He was right about something: there was a big difference in being a friend and being more. With Kevin I knew what a real friend looked like in a man. I wasn't going to allow Loyal to claim something he didn't deserve.

Chapter 18

I spent the next day with my two best friends. It was a welcomed distraction from thinking about Loyal or the mess that I had waiting whenever I decided to actually talk to him. As the day went on I found it hard to hide my feelings. I thought not talking to him would be the worst, but knowing that my phone hadn't rung all day was even worse. Not only did he hurt me but he hadn't tried to call or text me to give me a reason as to why he did.

The whipped cream in my coffee had completely melted into my cup. I watched as the remaining white color created its own art against the light brown coffee. I smiled. I loved finding art in the simple things of life.

"I was offered Australia."

Kevin's voice brought me out of my trance. He walked back to the table putting his phone down before sitting down.

"That's great, Kev." I smiled. I noticed he wasn't smiling back. "What's wrong?"

"I think I might need to stay around a little longer." Kevin stared at his phone screen.

I looked at Kevin and Bianca. Their serious faces let me know exactly why he was considering staying. I realized the whole day had gone by and Bianca hadn't mentioned her upcoming wedding at all. My friends were in protective mode.

"Take the job, Kevin. I will be just fine." I put my hand on top of his hand.

"I could really use the break."

"No, Kevin, you have wanted Australia for as long as I can remember and a little drama isn't going to keep you away from bringing me back a shot glass, boomerang, and koala bear. I will be fine, guys. In fact"—I stood up and motioned for the waitress to bring the check—"I am feeling really good about everything. So I fell for the wrong person, it happens. If anything, I know how to fall and get back up. And I have a hefty little check coming my way that means I can get back up in style."

The impossible happened: I actually convinced my two overprotective friends that I was okay. But in truth I wasn't okay. I was hurting more than any breakup I'd had before. I felt like I had lost one of my closest friends. There was a constant debate going on in my head. As much as I wanted to hear from him, a big piece of me didn't.

Back at my place I listened to Kevin making his preparations for Australia over the phone. I typed away on my computer. Maybe a vacation was what I needed. I hadn't seen any of the amazing places that Kevin had been. I still hadn't used the passport I got years ago when I had the idea to backpack across Europe for art inspiration. The idea quickly faded when I realized I had bills that needed to be paid.

I looked at some of the closer destinations I could go. I knew Bianca would buy her ticket instantly at the thought of us going to an island somewhere. A piece of me wanted to be alone. A week in Jamaica or Mexico on a secluded island where I felt like I was alone sounded like paradise to my ears.

"What are you doing?" Kevin appeared in my doorway.

"Just contemplating an escape from reality."

Kevin walked over and looked at my computer screen. "I think a vacation is a great idea. There are some pretty cool places I can recommend in Jamaica and Mexico for you. I think you would love Fiji though; it's got some amazing secluded villas and waterfalls."

"Oh you know me so well."

My phone rang. My whole body froze as I saw his face appear on the screen. Knowing that Kevin had to be looking at me, I pressed ignore and started typing in Fiji in the search bar.

"I never thought about Fiji. Oh do they have any of those huts that are completely surrounded by water?"

Kevin's protective stance quickly faded. He started rambling about various places in Fiji he knew I would love. His voice started to sound more and more like garble as thoughts of Loyal filled my head. Why was he calling now? Maybe he figured the smoke had cleared and I wasn't as upset. I needed answers but knew I wouldn't be able to get any until after Kevin was flying the friendly skies toward Australia.

I watched my friend packing his duffle bag by rolling his clothes one by one in a tight, perfect roll. He was meticulous with the way he packed, finding a way to fit everything he needed in the one duffle bag.

"Kevin, do you ever think about settling down with someone?"

Kevin laughed. "I'm a lone wolf, baby." He hit his hand against his chest.

"I'm serious."

Kevin turned away from his packing. "I've thought about it, but I love what I am doing right now and I'm not ready to give it up. How fair would it be for me to date someone when I am never in one place? Even right now all my furniture is in storage because I didn't see the need of keeping an apartment when I am never home."

"But don't you get lonely?"

"Not really, and if I do I'm sure I can find some lovely lady to spend a little time with wherever I am." Kevin winked.

I threw my pillow at him. "I don't think I'm ever going to find true love." I sighed. "I don't think if I ever did find it I would know what it really was."

"I think we all have that fear," Kevin said as he sat on my bed.

"It's too much work. I think I'd rather travel the world like you. See new things, do my art. That's what I'd love to do."

"Well do it then. The only thing stopping you is yourself, Rayne. You are single, no children, no relationship, and you are old enough to do whatever you want."

"And spend my time traveling the world like you." I smiled.

Kevin had his serious look on his face. "Rayne, you have always been your biggest critic. From your art to the weight you say you want to lose. You stand in your own way."

His words sliced me like a knife. I didn't want to admit that he was right. I'd always wanted to lose weight but let the fear of being in a gym with others or hurting myself stop me from doing what I needed to do. I now had the money to travel like I'd wanted to do but couldn't help but think about what I might miss out on if I stayed.

"I think it's time I make some changes, for real this time." I smiled.

A bright smile appeared on Kevin's face. He held his hand out. I put my hand in his and he squeezed tight.

"Who knows, maybe after we both achieve our dreams we can just get old and marry each other." The thought made us both laugh.

We fell asleep again in each other's arms. It was what I needed. I didn't want nor need sex from him, just the affection of having someone I knew truly cared about me was by my side.

Chapter 19

It was a teary good-bye as I dropped Kevin off at the airport. We hugged each other one last time before he disappeared into the Memphis terminal.

I headed home with my mind set to specific purpose. I wanted to get away, but I wanted there to be a purpose to it. My mind drifted to Paris. As an artist the Louvre was a place at the top of my bucket list. Thoughts of spending a week in Paris, studying the art and the culture sounded like an amazing trip and great way for me to actually make it about more than just escaping from life.

I didn't want anything changing my mind. One phone call to Bianca and she already had her doctor father drawing up paperwork for me to take an extended leave of absence from work. I wasn't going to return to the scene of the crime. I didn't need nor want to see Loyal and I didn't particularly want to hear people tell me over and over how I should have won the contest.

I picked up a bottle of wine and a meal before heading home. Even I was amazed at how motivated I was. It only took being around my motivated friend to boost my confidence enough to do something I'd always dreamed of doing.

I walked into the back door of my quiet apartment and set my food down on my kitchen countertop. I heard a faint knocking in the distance. The sound grew as I made my way to the front door. I peered through the peephole.

There stood Loyal with a bag in his hand.

My heart raced as I leaned against the wall. I didn't know if I should open the door or just play like I wasn't at home.

"Rayne, I heard your footsteps."

Fuck . . .

I took a deep breath and unlocked the door. I set it in my mind that there was nothing this man could say to me to make me forgive him for what he did.

Loyal walked in and stood directly in front of me. I knew he must have freshly sprayed cologne on as his familiar scent hit me the moment I opened the door. He looked good, so good I had to shake my head to stop myself from dreaming about more.

"Hey." His voice echoed through my hallway.

I didn't respond. I couldn't figure out what I actually wanted to say.

"Can we?" Loyal motioned to art space. I nodded my head as I followed him.

The space was very different. All of the art was gone and there was just a bare table where the sculpture used to sit. I sat on the edge of my couch as Loyal walked around the room.

"Man, I can't believe everything is gone. I guess it's time for you to fill it with some new work."

Loyal's smile fell on my very straight face. I didn't need the pleasantries. I folded my arms and waited to hear what he was going to say next.

"I got you something." Loyal held up the paper gift bag.

He walked over and handed me the gift. A piece of me didn't want to open it, but the curious side overrode it. I pulled a little statue out of the bag. It was a trophy. I read the plaque. It said Best Artist in the World. The ice was trying to melt. I put the trophy on the couch and folded my arms again.

"So it's like that?" Loyal nodded his head.

"How is it supposed to be, Loyal? You really think you can walk in here and act like there isn't anything wrong? Get the fuck outta here with that shit!"

"What is wrong, Rayne? I haven't done anything wrong."

I jumped up. "You have the nerve to show up here after you brought that chick to my fucking gallery opening. My most important night ever and you tried to ruin it for me."

"Whoa. First off I didn't bring her; she just happened to show up when I did. Second even if I did it doesn't matter; we have gone over this. I told you the business before you got—"

I threw my hand up to his face. "Stop! Before you fix your mouth to say what you are about to say let me correct you. Yes, you have told me from jump what the business is and I have always respected that. But you also said you are my friend. And as my friend you shouldn't want to do anything that you know will hurt me. I told you how I felt about that girl. You knew from when I promised you the damn ticket. But you walk in with her and spend the whole fucking night with her. As the guy I fuck with, no, you didn't have to care, but as my friend you should have!"

I was fuming. I wanted to throw something at him to make him feel the pain I felt in that moment. I wanted to see that he cared in his face but I didn't see a trace of remorse. He stood there just shaking his head.

"I told you we never should have slept together. I told you that you were going to fall for me."

I stared at the man who I'd let into my life so easily. He didn't look as shiny and perfect as he usually looked to me. I wanted to laugh but there wasn't anything funny about the situation.

"You are so missing the point." I shook my head.

"No, you are. I told you what happens when I fuck someone. I told you that you were going to fall and I

even told you I would never be your man. Yet here we are
arguing like a damn couple when I don't owe you shit. Did
you see me acting crazy when you were hugged up with ol'
dude at the exhibit? I didn't even care when that Shazza
Zulu–looking dude was at your house. Why? Because you
don't owe me shit and I'm not jealous."

"Shazza Zulu?"

"Yeah, you know Shazza who dated Freddie on *A
Different World.*"

I couldn't help it. We both erupted into laugher at his
statement. I felt the ice breaking. It was the little things
that made me like him. In a moment of pure heated
intensity he still found a way to make me laugh. But just
as usual once the laugher died down I was faced with the
reality of the situation.

"Loyal, you are right about one thing: I did foolishly
fall for you. That is something I can't take back even if I
wanted to. But just so you know, it was never the dick that
caused me to fall. No, sir, I was fucked from the moment
you walked into my office."

I sat back down on the side of the couch. I took a deep
breath. The truth was I was in love with the man standing
a few feet away from me and there was nothing that I
could do about it. I stared at a blank canvas sitting on the
ground behind Loyal.

"The mistake I made was not sleeping with you. The
mistake I made was believing that you actually valued me
as a friend. The sex stuff was secondary to the fact that I
thought I had someone who cared about me as a person
and as a friend. If that is the way you treat your friends,
your enemies are fucked."

Loyal took a step back. He wouldn't take his eyes off
of me. I knew he could see it in my face that I was done.
There was nothing he could say or do that would change
the fact that I would never look at him in the same light

I used to. I glanced at a blank canvas on the floor behind him.

"My life was just like that before I met you." I pointed at the blank canvas. "I was just here, blank. That's why I let you in so easy. I was ready for some color in my life and you provided that for me. I foolishly thought I had someone who not only I could experience some new things with but who would be there for me as a friend. Because in the end I never would have been able to allow you to do the things you have done to me if I didn't completely trust you."

I sighed. All things were coming into perspective for me.

"But you know what, no matter how much color you provided, in the end it's just a bunch of splatter on a canvas. You and me never made real art," I said as I put the trophy back in the bag he gave it to me in.

"Yeah, but some of the most popular paintings in the world are just splashes of paint and scribble on a canvas. I think we make great art together. Just like in art it's all in the eye of the person who is looking at it."

I looked up to see a semi smile on Loyal's face. He walked up to me and put his hands on my shoulders. "Rayne, I apologize if you felt that I hurt you at the event. That wasn't my intention." Loyal massaged my shoulders with his big hands. His touch sent chills down my spine. "I do value you as a friend and I don't want you to think that I don't. I do love you, Rayne. I got nothing but love for my beautiful artist."

"Yeah, well having love for me is not going to change what you did. I will never look at you the same, Loyal. There's no fixing that."

Loyal shook his head. "I disagree. I'm sorry, Rayne, but just like I said in the beginning you aren't going anywhere. I refuse to let you. You are my friend and I'm not willing to lose you as a friend, no matter what you say right now."

I stood up. "You can't control that." I stood still as he walked in front of me.

"I can control it, because I'm not going to allow you to leave my life. I might have some major making up to do, but in the end I'm not letting you go."

Loyal put both of his hands on each side of my face, pulling me close to him. I closed my eyes as his lips pressed against mine. I didn't know why I was allowing it, but I couldn't pull away.

It was as though our whole relationship was flashing through my mind during that kiss. I never should have let him in but I did. He held a piece of me that I wanted to let go of, but the truth was no matter what my mouth said, I still wanted him there.

I felt my hands rise as they wrapped around Loyal's muscular frame. I held him tight, hoping to feel something that would let me know that the words he was speaking were true. I wanted to believe him, but in my mind I knew it was bullshit. He would say whatever he needed to say to keep me. I just didn't understand why. I forced my arms to let go, pushing my body away from his.

"Why? Why are you so determined to keep me around when you have Kelis and the rest of your women?"

Loyal's eyes gleaming down on me made my body tense up. I prepared myself for whatever amazing line he was going to come up with. I knew it was going to be poetic, something to make me go weak in the knees whenever I thought about it again. He was going to put down his best pimpin' in this moment, simply because he knew it was the only way he was going to keep me in the end.

"You really want to know why?" Loyal didn't take his eyes off of me.

I nodded my head, prepared for the ultimate revelation.

Loyal took a step back. He looked at me up and down. "Because," Loyal said.

I was confused. Where was the grand reason? "What do you mean because?"

"Because, Rayne. That is the reason. I want you in my life because I do. There isn't anything bigger than that. Me wanting you here is reason enough."

I stood there wondering what next. Did I accept his simple answer or did I tell him to hit the road? My eyes searched for more in his eyes but there wasn't. It was really that simple. The truth was Loyal would never be loyal to me, but he for some reason wanted to keep me in his life. He made me feel unlike anyone had ever made me feel before. The bad thing was it was either overwhelmingly wonderful, or horrible. There was no middle ground.

"Rayne," Loyal breathed my name. I loved the way it sounded.

He breathed my name again, and again until I finally answered.

"Do you want me to leave?" His raspy voice was haunting me.

"I want you to say something more than what you said. Because . . . That's not a reason."

"Rayne." Loyal put his hands back on my face. I wanted to cry but the tears just wouldn't form. "Rayne."

No words, no tears. I was numb and there was nothing that I could say to get him to give me a better answer.

"Do you want me to leave?"

Loyal's words filled my mind. The answer should have been simple. He not only hadn't given me anything that I could really work with but in the end I knew I would never get a better answer. On the other hand just having his hands on my face made my flesh crave him more.

"Do you want me to leave?" he repeated.

"I don't know because I—"

"Rayne." Loyal pulled me closer. He wrapped his hands around my body planting one single kiss on the right side of my neck. I could feel his breath on the top of my ear. "For once in your life stop overanalyzing everything and tell me, with just the first word that pops in your mind, do you want me to leave?"

I closed my eyes and took a deep breath. There was only thing that came to mind.

My head hit my pillow. Loyal's tongue devoured my breasts as he held them with his usual forceful touch. I closed my eyes as he entered me. The pleasurable pain took over my body, filling any holes that were left empty from the past weekend.

I kept my eyes closed as he fucked me hard. I could hear the voices of Pashun and Kevin in my head. I knew it was wrong, and I knew I deserved something more than what he was giving me. But I knew that in that moment I would rather have him than go back to having nothing at all. 'Cause in the end, any color on a canvas is better than no color at all.

About the Author

Skyy is a 27-year-old author, screenwriter, and playwright and self proclaimed weirdo from Memphis, TN. Her first novel, *Choices* was originally released in 2007 and quickly gained popularity both within the gay and lesbian community and within the urban fiction community. The highly anticipated sequel, *Consequences*, was released in 2009 and rocketed to the top 10 lesbian bestsellers list on Amazon.com and at independent bookstores across the country. Skyy and her books were featured on the nationally syndicated radio show, *The Michael Baisden Show*. In Skyy's spare time she enjoys traveling, watching and spending a crazy amount of money on DVDS, and chatting with fans on online.

Contact Skyy
www.simplyskyy.com
skyy@simplyskyy.com
www.facebook.com/simplyskyy
www.twitter.com/simplyskyy

You Only Live Once

by

Treasure Hernandez

Chapter 1

"Come on, ladies. Both of my girls cannot back out on me," Dakota said as she sat at a downtown Flint, Michigan restaurant looking over the lunch menu with her besties, Shyla and Trice. "I would have never even agreed to represent my company at that stupid insurance conference if I had known you two were going to bail out on me. I only agreed to do it because I figured I could turn a paid, out-of-town business trip into a fun three nights and four days of pleasure with my girlfriends."

Shyla slightly lowered her menu that had been covering her entire face. It was now low enough just to where her eyes could be seen. She looked over the menu at Dakota. "Girl, please. Trice and I would have fun. You, missy, would be all day in seminars, meetings, and workshops."

"Yeah, but afterward I could kick it with you two," Dakota said.

"No, afterward you will complain about how tired you are from being in seminars all day, take you a shower, order room service, and climb into bed and cuddle up to some reality show all night while Trice and I kick it." Shyla sucked her teeth and went back to skimming her menu.

"Now you know that is not true. I would never have you guys go all the way out to Vegas and not kick it and have fun with y'all."

Trice, their other partner in crime, chimed in. "Dakota Marie Smith, please. We've all been friends for what, six, seven years? We know what fun means to you. And it's not what it means to us." She pointed to herself and Shyla. "Ya heard?" She chuckled, then directed her next comment to Shyla. "I don't even know why we allowed Little Bo Peep in our clique in the first place. We are all clearly not cut from the same cloth."

"And what's that supposed to mean?" Dakota tried not to snap, but clearly her question was laced with a snappy undertone.

"Slow your roll, girlfriend." Trice put her hand up. "Pump your breaks. All I'm saying is that"—she looked Dakota up and down—"you're a black girl named Dakota. That don't even sound like fun."

Shyla burst out laughing. She continued to laugh until Dakota sharply turned her head in her direction and shot her an evil look.

"I can't help it that my name is Dakota," she replied. "Blame it on my white mother. She's the one who named me."

"Oh, but your father could have stepped in at any minute and used his black card to put a stop to that nonsense," Shyla said as she and Trice laughed and high-fived.

"You know what?" Dakota said in a controlled soft, uppity-like voice. "Fuck you, and fuck you." She turned her attention back to her menu and then threw in, "And, consider yourselves lucky that that was in my white girl voice."

Trice play-hit Dakota on the shoulder and they all laughed. The women looked over their menus for a couple more minutes until their waiter came and took their orders.

While they waited for their food to come out, Dakota decided to use the time to try to convince her girls to join her on her trip to Las Vegas. Her company was paying both Dakota's hotel and airfare, so there would be no out-of-pocket expense on her part. Even the food and transportation expenses during her stay in Vegas could be expensed.

"All you guys have to do is pay your airfare," Dakota reasoned. "The hotel is paid for by the company. It's a room at the Rio. I went online and checked it out and that hotel is PP: plush and posh. I have a double room and the couch has a pullout bed. We can even upgrade to a two-bedroom suite if you guys want and split the difference three ways. Come on," Dakota whined.

"I promise you, D, if my vacation time had been approved, I'd be there; you know that, ma," Trice said. "But one of the members of my team beat me to the punch. She literally put in her vacation time two days before I requested mine. She's off that entire week and my team leader needs me, so mine wasn't approved. You know darn well you would not have to ask me twice to join you in Vegas otherwise. Come on, now. Vegas. Sin City. What goes on in Vegas stays in Vegas. Puhleaze! I wouldn't miss that for the world."

"Right," Shyla agreed. "And if I even had the vacation time, I would have taken the days off to join you in Vegas in a heartbeat. When I told you I would go with you, I had no idea I'd used up all my vacation time. A chick only has one day left."

"Well, I'm not surprised you only have one vacation day left. I'm surprised you have any." Trice rolled her eyes. "Every time you meet some guy at the club, you spend the entire night talking to him until last call. Somehow you end up talking until the wee hours of the morning at the Waffle House, getting to know him because he could be the one."

Dakota chuckled at Trice's sarcasm and then listened as Trice continued.

"The next morning you're too damn tired to go to work so you call off; and if Mr. The One is lucky, you spend that day up under his ass," Trice said all in one breath. "So yeah, I can see why you are out of vacation days."

Shyla just looked at Trice for a second before saying, "Fuck you. And that was in my hood voice."

Again, the women shared a laugh.

"Y'all are right." Dakota figured it was fine time to agree with her girls on at least one thing after seeing the way those two get turnt up. "I have no idea how I got caught up with you two. We are not even made up from the same kind of pattern, let alone the same cloth. Y'all broads are crazy."

"See, ya just boring. You can't even cuss us out right," Trice said.

Shyla agreed. "That's the white girl in her, though. 'Cause, see, a one hundred percent black girl would have said, 'Y'all bitches are crazy,'" Shyla said.

"I disagree," Dakota begged to differ. "Oprah is one hundred percent black and she does not use the word bitch outside of her acting role in *The Butler*." Dakota was dead serious.

"Calm down, Pooh Bear, you know I was just joking," Shyla said.

By now, both Trice and Shyla had been friends with Dakota long enough to know that it took only two things to set their friend off and to get her up on her soapbox. One was taking a stab at her mixed heritage and the other was her weight. Ironically, the girls had given Dakota the nickname of Pooh Bear because they said her skin complexion, her chubby figure, and her soft, lovable tone and calm demeanor reminded them so much of the Disney character. Since their pet name for her was all in love, and Dakota knew her girls loved her and would never try to take advantage of her sensitive areas, the name Pooh

Bear didn't bother her at all. As a matter of fact, she loved the term of endearment her girls had given her. But let anyone else call her to the carpet with that ol' "What are you?" or "What are you mixed with?" crap, or even that "You have such a pretty face," and it was on and popping.

If ever a guy stepped to Dakota with that lame "I like 'em thick," or "I like big girls" line, Dakota dismissed them with the quickness. Trice had the pleasure of witnessing a dismissal herself.

"Girl, his ass was fine. Why did you kick him to the curb like that?" Trice had asked the first time she saw Dakota send a guy to the left for using one of those pickup lines. *"And he said he liked 'em thick."* Trice slapped Dakota's derrière. *"And you thick. So what was the problem?"*

"The problem is that a real man who just wanted me would have only seen me," Dakota explained. *"He wouldn't have seen all my skin or the color of it. He would have just seen a beautiful woman he wanted to get with. Period."* She looked at Trice. *"Just like with your dark skin. How many dudes have you had to cuss out for using that stupid line, 'You so cute to be dark skinned?' Why can't you just be cute? Why the extra?"*

"Yeah, you're right. I can't stand that ol' color-struck shit." Trice nodded. *"I guess I never looked at it that way."*

"Well, it's the same thing with me. Either a dude is going to see a beautiful woman he wants to get to know because of just that: she's a beautiful woman he wants to get to know. Or he can keep it moving. And the fact that guys even think what they are saying is a compliment only makes them that much more of a jerk."

"Say no more." Trice put her hand up. *"I feel you and I got your back."*

And her girls had had Dakota's back ever since, which was why she was so upset about the fact that they wouldn't be joining her in Vegas to have her back while there.

The waiter brought the girls' food, made sure they had everything they needed, then left them to dig into their lunch specials. And everyone did with the exception of Dakota, who just sat there picking at her food.

"You acting like a preschooler who just got served carrots as a snack," Shyla said to Dakota. "Girl, eat."

Trice looked at her watch. "Yeah, we have to be back at work soon."

Although the girls worked in different departments and on different teams, they each worked for the same insurance company. The three girls had all been working for the same company for the exact same amount of time. It was during training when they all actually met each other. Before that day six and a half years ago, none of the girls had known one another.

During the six weeks of training they became close, sharing lunch together each day. Once training was over, at first they were all on the same team, but over the years, due to promotions and transfers, they eventually ended up in different departments in the company. That didn't change the fact that they'd become three peas in a pod and had experienced almost every memorable moment in their lives together since.

Dakota covered her face with her hands. "I know we have to get back to work, but I have lost my appetite. I'm just sad you guys aren't coming to Vegas with me. I have never been to Vegas before and now here I'm going all by my lonesome. To be honest, hell, I'm scared."

"Awwwww," both Shyla and Trice said then each reached around the round table to hug Dakota, who sat between the two.

"Our Pooh Bear has to finally venture off into the forest without us," Shyla said in cooing voice.

"And how I'm going to miss Tigger and Piglet." Dakota sighed, putting her elbow on the table and then placing her chin in her hand.

"Hey, who's Tigger and who's Piglet?" Shyla said, then looked down at each hip. "I know I done picked up a little weight, but damn, why I gotta be Piglet? Why can't a ho be Christopher Columbus?"

"Girl, you mean Christopher Robin," Trice said and then broke out in laughter.

"Well, whatever, Winnie-the-Pooh's human buddy in the forest." Shyla rolled her eyes.

"Ugh, I'm sitting here sick that my BFFs aren't going to Vegas with me and you all are arguing of what character I'm naming you from a Walt Disney story. Really?" Dakota huffed.

"You'll be okay," Trice said, rubbing Dakota's back. "Just look at the bright side; now you can change the room to a king. You'll have that king bed all to yourself to curl up in at night and watch television."

Both Shyla and Trice couldn't help laughing again. Dakota pushed the women off of her, looked at them each, and said, "Fuck both you bitches. And that was in my black voice."

Chapter 2

"My baby is going off to Vegas all by herself. I don't know if I'm ready for that," Mr. Smith said as he, his wife, and two daughters sat at the dinner table.

"Dad, I'm so not a baby," Dakota said before taking in a bite of rigatoni, her favorite dish that her mother prepared. "I'm twenty-five. Hello."

"Yeah, well you're still my baby." Mr. Smith looked from one daughter to the next. "Both of you are."

"Oh, Lord," said Billie, Dakota's older sister by two years. "Don't get him started. It was only just last year I had to stop calling him to let him know when I'd gotten in for the night whenever I go out."

Mrs. Smith chuckled. "Come on, girls, y'all know how y'all's father is. He watches too much of that ID Channel mess. Worries himself sick thinking the worst."

"Can you blame me?" Mr. Smith asked. "This world is crazy. And to have the two most beautiful daughters in the world on top of that. How do you expect a man to sleep at night knowing his daughter is out there in the streets? No, sir. I couldn't rest until I knew Billie was back in the comfort and safety of her own home."

Dakota swallowed her food and thought for a minute. "That's strange, Daddy. I don't recall you ever having me check in at night with a phone call."

"That's because he knows you are right at home in bed watching *Love & Hip Hop*." Billie laughed. "You are the last person to be out on the streets getting into

something. I can hear your phone call to Daddy now."
Billie put her hand to her ear, pretending it was a phone,
and began to mock Dakota. "Dad, I had the most daring
night ever. I went to the bathroom during commercial
break and I flushed a wipey down the toilet and stood
there and waited for the toilet to flood over." She began
clapping in excitement.

Dakota dropped her fork, clearly offended. "So are you
trying to say I'm boring?"

"Oh no," Billie said making a serious face. "I'm sure I
could go on the Internet right now and find people other
than you who feel that watching paint dry should be a
sport." Billie burst out laughing.

"Honey, stop," Mrs. Smith ordered. "You're upsetting
your sister."

And upset Dakota surely was. "For your information,
I know how to have fun. I'm not boring," she snapped.
But did she really? Could everyone be wrong? Because,
just two days ago at lunch with Shyla and Trice, Dakota
had heard basically the same thing from them. Now, her
sister? Could it have been true? Was she really the boring
girl who did nothing but go to work every day and, for
fun, watch television? Dakota never saw herself that way.
She'd hit the club scene with Trice and Shyla every now
and then. Sure it had to be someone's birthday or some
other special occasion, but she'd go nonetheless. And
she seemed to have fun as far as she was concerned. But
clearly what was fun to her wasn't fun to everybody else.

"Your sister is not trying to call you boring," Mrs.
Smith interjected. "Are you, Billie?" She looked to her
oldest daughter, shooting her a look that said "you better
line up or else."

Billie took a swig of her apple Snapple. "Absolutely not.
I'm not trying to say it at all. I am saying it." She took
another sip.

"Forget you," Dakota said. "Just because I don't run the streets does not mean I'm boring."

"It doesn't mean you're the life of the party either," Billie retorted. "Come on, sis, seriously. List the last five things you did that were really fun and exciting, daring, or even risk-taking?"

Dakota thought for a minute.

"Go ahead. I'm waiting."

Dakota was still thinking.

"See, just what I thought." Billie shook her head and took a bite of her mother's famous rigatoni, a family favorite and recipe of their mother's grandmother, the girls' Italian great-grandmother.

"Hold up." Dakota put her hand up. "Give me a second."

"Child, if it takes that long to come up with something fun and exciting that you've done, then it ain't even worth mentioning. You're only twenty-five years old for Christ's sake. Stuff should be rolling off your tongue. You're in the prime of fun. After twenty-five, folks tend to hold you more accountable for the stuff you do." Billie shook her head. "Wasted years."

Eager to prove her sister wrong, Dakota began rambling off a few things. "Just last week I went to this amazing bachelorette party."

"Oh, you mean the one you said you excused yourself from and stayed in the bathroom the entire time the strippers were there?" Billie held up an L with her index finger and thumb and made a buzzing sound as if Dakota was on a game show and had gotten the answer wrong.

Dakota thought of something else, quickly. "Well, Trice and Shyla and I just had a girl's night out. We went to see *The Best Man Holiday* and had dinner afterward. We talked and laughed so much about that movie that the waitress at the restaurant had to come over and give us a warning for being too loud."

Billie feigned a tremble. "Oooohh. 'Lions, tigers, bears, oh my!' That must have been so scary. Dakota's waitress warned her for laughing too loud."

"Screw you!" Dakota snapped. She'd had enough of her smart-alecky sister.

"Hey, watch your mouth," Mr. Smith said.

"Awww, sookie-sookie." Billie smiled. "Miss Dakota might have a little fire in her after all. Hmmm, perhaps there is another side to Little Miss Muffet."

Dakota slammed her fist down on the table. "I am not about to be referred to as one more nursery rhyme character." A couple days ago she was Little Bo Peep and now she was Little Miss Muffet.

"Young lady, I don't know what has your feathers all ruffled, but your mother has taken the time to prepare a farewell dinner for you since you'll be leaving for Vegas in a few days. Is this behavior how you thank her?" He looked from Dakota to Billie. "And you're not off the hook either. Why you insist on antagonizing your sister, I have no idea. Now you both need to apologize to your mother right now then help with the kitchen."

Dakota and Billie both had regretful looks on their faces. "Sorry, Mom," they mumbled simultaneously.

"What? I couldn't understand either of you," Mr. Smith said with sternness. "And if I couldn't understand you, then neither could she."

"Sorry, Mom," they both said loud and clearly.

Mrs. Smith nodded her acceptance of their apologies.

Dinner was pretty quiet after that point. After everyone was finished eating, Mr. Smith and Mrs. Smith retreated to the living room to watch some television while Dakota and Billie cleared the table and went to clean up the kitchen. The first few minutes of that were done in silence as well. But after so long, Dakota couldn't take it anymore. She had to ask her sister what had been on her mind ever since their argument at the dinner table.

"Billie?" Dakota said as she swept the kitchen floor.

"Yeah," Billie replied, still acting like she had an attitude with Dakota for getting them in trouble with their
father; just like old times.

"Am I really boring?"   .

Billie didn't hesitate. "Hell, yeah. I know you're my kid
sister and most older siblings don't like their younger
ones to be tagging along, but you were the epitome of why
I didn't want my kid sister tagging along. You'd whine
and try to talk me out of anything daring and exciting."

"That was only to protect you. I didn't want you getting
into any trouble."

"No one goes through life without ever getting into
trouble, Dakota."

Dakota looked down as if guilty as charged. She honestly couldn't recall five times she'd gotten in trouble any
more than she could recall the last five fun and exciting
things she'd done.

"At least no normal person goes through life without
ever getting into trouble. Girl, you made me look so bad
growing up. Because you did nothing wrong, everything
I did do was colossal in Mommy's and Daddy's eyes. I
mean, you're worse than some of those Christians I work
with. Even some of them cuss, listen to Kendrick Lamar,
and go out for drinks with their girls every now and then."

"I cuss."

"Yeah, but usually only in a setting and under circum-
stances to prove to people that you can be edgy if pushed.
It's not natural for you. Cuss words don't even sound
right coming out of your mouth. You don't really drink
when out. And then when you do drink it's them little
cutesy drinks. Girl, get you a rum and Coke, a gin and
juice . . . something! And you have the smooth listening
contemporary station locked in on your car radio dial. I
can hardly even stay awake around you." She shook her

head. "To this day, I have no idea how you, Trice, and Shayla have been friends for so long. Now them two . . ." Billie's face lit up. "I can kick it with them all night. They are my kind of girls. I can't even picture the three of you out at the club. What do you do? Hold their purses while they dance?"

Dakota immediately stopped sweeping and looked at her sister with hurt in her eyes. "Really, Billie?"

"What?" Billie thought for a minute. "Oh, Dakota, please." She unsympathetically shooed her hand at her younger sister. "I didn't mean it like that and you know it. So if you are trying to make it out as though I'm trying to say the big girl always sits around and holds purses, that's not even where I was going with that."

Dakota had to be honest with herself. She knew that's not what her sister meant. Even though Dakota was a size eighteen and Billie was a six, Billie's entire clique was bigger than her, so she knew that Billie was the last person on earth to stereotype big girls.

"Tara is bigger than you and she's my best friend. And not only is Tara my best friend, but she is the epitome of fun and a good time. You say you are comfortable with the skin you are in and who you are, and I'd like to believe you. But, Dakota, I really think you let the whole weight thing keep you from living. And you're not even that big."

Dakota growled. "Ooooh, I hate when people say that to me." Dakota mocked, "'You're not that big.' Well damn it, I'm bigger than you."

"So what? A person's size shouldn't keep them from living." She looked her sister up and down, then stopped her eyes. With deep sincerity Billie said, "I love you, sissy. But the fact that you have all these little pet peeves about your weight or race, or whatever, means that sometimes it's more of an issue for you than it is for the rest of the world. So here." Billie took the broom out of Dakota's hands, leaned it against the counter, then took Dakota by the hands and led her into the bathroom.

Billie turned on the light and then positioned Dakota in front of the mirror.

"What?" Dakota shrugged, trying to figure out her sister's point.

"For once, why don't you just look at yourself and see something else? Don't see your size, complexion, or anything else this crazy society tries to make you think is important. You want the rest of the world to see something else, but you yourself won't even do it, so, baby sister"—Billie turned Dakota to face her—"promise me something."

Dakota nodded trying to hold back a tear.

"When you go to Vegas, from the minute that plane lands, the world has no mirrors. Never mind what you've seen or what you feel other people have seen when they've looked at you. It's all null and void. The only stranger you will meet is yourself. The Dakota who's standing right here in front of me, leave her on that plane. I repeat: she is not going on this trip with you."

Dakota was slightly confused. "What do you mean?"

"I mean, dare to get off that plane in Vegas and introduce yourself as someone else, someone you don't even know. Let her be free. Let her just be. You don't know what she looks like, what she's been through, what she feels like. All you know is that she just is. That's the same thing you're always preaching you want other people to see when they look at you. You don't want people trying to figure out 'what you are' or 'what you are mixed with' or 'what size you wear.' So you don't do it either. I bet if you can strip yourself of all that, underneath it all is someone who has been dying to have a little fun." Billie winked.

"But, Billie—"

"No buts, damn it. Just do it. Just live. For once in your life say 'hello' to someone new. Something new. Something different." Billie turned Dakota back to face herself in the mirror. "And say good-bye to her."

Chapter 3

As Dakota sat on the plane to Vegas she still couldn't believe the only things she'd taken were the clothes on her back. *How did I ever allow my crazy sister to talk me into this?* she asked herself as she stared out of the plane's window.

"What about my underwear?" Dakota had asked Billie who sat on her bed watching her gather the bare minimum necessities to take on the trip.

"Nope." Billie shook her head. "Get new underwear too. Not the underwear Dakota would wear either. Because remember, Dakota is not going to Vegas with you. No need to buy her a damn thing."

Dakota stared into her carry-on bag. "What about my bath and body products? My smell goods?"

"Nope. That's stuff Dakota wears. Remember, the theme is something new."

Dakota threw her hands up and let them fall freely back down to her side. "This is crazy. I'm checking in a completely empty suitcase and a carry-on with nothing but"—she looked through the carry-on—"a toothbrush, toothpaste and deodorant." She shook her head. "I can't."

"I know you can't. That's why you're not going to Vegas. The stranger in you is going." Billie threw her hands together in excitement. "Isn't this great? It's like a Lifetime movie or something isn't it? Wallflower plans a trip to Vegas but blooms into a rose when she gets there?"

Dakota watched her sister bounce on the bed in glee. "Well, I'm glad you're excited about this. I'm scared to death," Dakota admitted.

"You said it yourself; you were scared to go without your girls anyway. So what's the difference?" Billie stood up and rested her hands on Dakota's shoulders. "Come on, sis. You can do it. Throw caution in the wind. Live on the wild side. Take advantage of being twenty-five years old, sexy, and single. I promise you won't regret it."

As Dakota now sat on the plane with her stomach in knots, she was already regretting it.

"Ma'am, I'm going to need you to push your seat all the way in its upright position and put your tray up," the stewardess said to Dakota.

She hadn't heard the initial request over the intercom because her mind had traveled back to her conversation with Billie earlier that day, prior to Billie taking her to the airport.

"We're about to land."

"Oh, okay. I'm sorry." Dakota smiled. "Thank you." Dakota pulled her seat all the way forward, put her snack tray up, held her breath, and prepared for landing.

Dakota truly didn't feel like herself once she stepped off that plane and entered the Las Vegas, Nevada airport. She felt more like Alice in Wonderland. If a person was truly trying to leave their old self behind and had never been to Vegas before, it wouldn't be as hard as it might seem. Heck, even if they had been to Las Vegas before it still couldn't have been that difficult. There was just something in the air there; something exciting, or as her sister would have put it, something new. She took a deep breath and inhaled whatever it was in the air. And Dakota truly felt brand new indeed.

As she walked toward baggage claim she looked around at all the people and heard the sounds and saw the blinking lights of the slot machines. She felt as if she was in a whole new world. What surprised her most was that she wasn't scared, not one bit. Her blood was pumping and her heart was beating faster than usual, but this was pure adrenaline. She was anxious to be a part of this piece of the world.

The people from different walks of life were buzzing about. Try as she might to find similarities between those she crossed paths with, she couldn't. Or, maybe that's just who Dakota was. She couldn't because that's not who she was; she didn't know how. She saw no cliques. No stereotypes. No one looked to be trying to fit in and, most importantly, she didn't fit in anywhere. No one fit in. Who were these people and where had they come from? Would she find anyone on this trip she'd be able to relate to, or who might be able to relate to her?

The only stranger you will meet is yourself. Her sister's words immediately came to mind. This wasn't about other people. This was all about her. Dakota allowed her sister's words to sink in; then she thought about how she could begin to put them in motion.

She cleared her throat, straightened up her shoulders, then with her head held high took her next step; her first step away from Dakota. The Dakota back in Flint would have held her head down and only focused her eyes on her path and the signs leading her to her destination, which was baggage claim. But this new Dakota, this perfect stranger, was just the opposite.

"Hello," Dakota said to a woman that looked to be heading to her departure gate.

The woman smiled and nodded.

Hmmm, that wasn't so bad, Dakota thought. Shyla was always talking to people she didn't know. One hello could turn into a half-hour conversation with a perfect stranger. She was just so free, so confident, so interesting. Dakota had always been envious of Shyla's ability to just strike up a conversation with someone. Now here she was, taking baby steps toward doing that same thing.

Passing by was a gentleman taking a bite out of a pretzel. He held a laptop case on the same arm as the hand he was using to eat the pretzel. In the other hand the man was rolling a small carry-on.

"Good afternoon." Dakota smiled.

The man did a double take, smiled, then returned the greeting. As rushed and preoccupied as the man appeared, no way had Dakota thought he would take the time to greet her, but he had. Not only that, but when she decided to look back at the man over her shoulder, he was returning the gesture.

"Oh my God," Dakota said under her breath as she quickly turned back around. "Oh goodness!" Dakota felt like she'd run into a brick wall. Instead it was a man who had been walking in front of her. Obviously while Dakota was admiring the man behind her, the one in front of her had halted his steps for some reason.

"I'm so sorry," Dakota apologized to the gentleman.

He turned around with his mouth opened, prepared to speak. For some reason his words got caught. He quickly recovered them though. "It's, ah, quite all right, Miss, Mrs. . . ." he fished.

"Just call me Dak . . . Marie." Dakota's insides were screaming, *why did you just do that?* while on the outside a smile was plastered on her face.

"Marie." The man extended his hand. "Nice to meet you, Marie. And apology accepted. By the way, I'm Leon," he said.

Dakota extended her hand. "Pleased to meet you, Leon." As Dakota finished up shaking Leon's hand, someone accidentally bumped her as they hurried by.

"Oh, I guess we shouldn't be standing in the middle of the Las Vegas airport of all places. Anyway, again, nice meeting you."

"Same here," Leon said, then began walking again.

It was just a little awkward with both Dakota and Leon walking side by side. Dakota was the one who decided to break the ice. "So do you live here in Vegas?"

"Oh, no," Leon replied.

"Here for business or pleasure?"

"That depends," Leon said.

Dakota nodded. Her insides were about to explode. Leon had just opened a door and she knew if she walked through it, things could get crazy. She hadn't been in Vegas for a good five minutes. Did she really want to get caught up before ever even leaving the airport? Absolutely not. She at least needed to plan out how she wanted to . . . *planning*. That was something Dakota would do, but her alter ego, Marie, wouldn't Marie be more of a fun, spur-of-the-moment type of chick? There was only one way to find out.

"Depends on what?" There, Dakota had walked through the door, or at least allowed Marie to do it. And Marie had left it open for whatever might follow.

"Depends on if I can find something else to get into besides business. Something that might be pleasurable." He looked Dakota up and down. "What about you? Is this the place you call home or are you here for business and/ or pleasure?"

"No, I live in the Midwest. As far as business or plea-sure"—she gave Leon the once-over—"I'm thinking both."

He made sure to look away from her so that she couldn't see the blushing in his eyes. It wasn't quick enough. For the first time in her life Dakota had actually made a man blush, or at least the first time she'd ever noticed or paid attention. She wasn't one that typically made eye contact. But Marie did . . . and she liked it.

Dakota had always been the one waiting on the other person to make the next move. But she was now realizing that making the first move set the pace and allowed the one setting the pace to be in control. If it made any sense and without sounding like an oxymoron, she wanted to lose control and be the one in control.

"So who knows?" Dakota continued, "Perhaps we both may end up engaging in a little pleasure."

"Without a doubt," Leon said.

Upon finally arriving at the baggage claim area, Leon and Dakota started to head their separate ways. Dakota's first stop before heading to get her suitcase was to the bathroom. She'd been holding it for the last half hour.

"Excuse me, Marie!" Leon called out to Dakota, who in turn kept looking around for the ladies' room. "Marie."

Dakota only turned to see what rude person was yelling out someone's name when she realized it was Leon trying to get her attention. Just that quickly she'd pushed her alter ego aside. She'd have to do better.

"Yes," Dakota replied, taking a step back toward Leon.

"With all the crazies that are in the world today, I know my chances might be slim," Leon stated with very little confidence, "but do you mind sharing with me where you are staying?"

The only thing that came to Dakota's mind were all of those real-life horror stories her father had shared with her from countless ID Channel shows he'd taken in. Leon must have seen the wheels of skepticism churning in Dakota's head.

"On second thought, why don't I just give you my number? I'll be in Vegas the next few days. If after you handle your business portion of the trip and you want to engage in a little pleasure—I don't know, dinner, a show, or what have you—please don't hesitate to reach out to me. Does that sound fine?"

Dakota exhaled. She was about to shoot down Leon's initial offer. No way was she going to tell him exactly what room he could come find her in in order to slice her up into a million tiny pieces. Now the latter offer was doable. Dakota removed her phone from her purse and took it off airplane mode. She then added Leon as a contact as he rattled off his phone number to her.

"Well, hopefully before my trip is up I will have heard from you," Leon said. "If not, I guess meeting you will be the most pleasure I have on this trip. Because the pleasure of meeting you has been all mine indeed." Leon smiled then headed toward his baggage claim carousels.

"OMG," Dakota said under her breath as she watched Leon walk away. "Lord, let him be real and not vanish away as if he's been nothing but a vision."

Dakota couldn't stand there too much longer to make sure Leon wasn't a figment of her imagination and would just poof away into thin air. If she did, she'd find herself standing in a puddle of her own bodily fluid. She looked up and around, finally spotting the women's restroom, and then made her way inside. There were just a couple people standing in line in front of her. While she waited her phone rang.

"Hey, Trice," Dakota answered after looking at the caller ID.

"Is my little Pooh Bear safe and sound in Vegas?" Trice cooed through the phone. "I feel like a mama whose baby bird just left the nest." She did a little fake cry.

"Trice, cut it out," Dakota said. "Yes, I'm here. Still at the airport. But I'm okay."

"How was your flight?"

"It was good. I just landed a few minutes ago." Dakota noticed she was next in line and she'd just heard a toilet flush. "Look, I'm in the restroom now. I'll check in with you later once I get settled into my room."

"All right, chick. I'll call Shyla and let her know you made it safe and sound."

"Thanks, Trice, and I'll talk to you guys later."

"All right, love you!"

"Love you too. Bye bye." Dakota couldn't hit the end button quick enough. She dang near knocked over the lady coming out of the bathroom stall running into it. "Sorry, ma'am," she apologized and then relieved herself just in the nick of time.

After handling her business in the restroom, Dakota made it over to her baggage carousel. Everyone else had dispersed. There was only one suitcase still circling around on the conveyor. Just as Dakota was about to go grab it off, an airline worker did so.

"Oh, that's mine," Dakota called out. "I had to make a pit stop in the bathroom, but I was coming to get it." She felt the need to explain herself for abandoning her suitcase.

"Oh, no problem," the gentleman said until he actually lifted the bag. Then he made the same strange face as the airline worker who had checked in her suitcase made.

"It's empty. I know," Dakota said, embarrassed. "I, uh, plan on uh, hitting the jackpot and doing some shopping." Once again she'd felt the need to explain herself, only with a lie this time.

The worker just smiled, nodded, and passed her bag to her.

"Thank you." Dakota smiled. Once the worker was out of face view she sighed and then rolled her eyes up into her head. "Lord, Billie, what did I let you talk me into?"

Chapter 4

The online pictures and reviews did not do Dakota's room at the Rio All Suites Las Vegas hotel justice. It was fabulous! The entire hotel was fabulous. It wasn't on the strip with all the other dozens of hotels, but had free shuttles to the strip if that's what the guests so desired. It felt more upscale, away from all the hustle and bustle and riffraff of the strip. Dakota hadn't really gotten to experience the strip besides her taxi ride from the airport to her hotel. But, she planned on experiencing every inch of Vegas that she could in the little bit of time she had.

But first things first; she had to get some shopping done. It was only noon Vegas time thanks to the three-hour time zone difference. The kickoff registration and reception for the conference wasn't until six that evening, so Dakota had plenty of time to go do a little shopping so that she'd at least have something to wear this evening and for tomorrow's seminar.

Not having any unpacking to do, Dakota went and opened her blinds to the beautiful Las Vegas skyline. Then just like she was doing a commercial promoting Vegas, she opened her arms wide and fell back on the king-sized bed.

"This is heaven!" she shouted out.

Dakota lay there for a minute, taking in the relaxation. She looked over at the nightstand where her eyes fixated on the remote. She went to grab it but then stopped herself. "No, no, no. That's something Dakota would do:

sit and watch television. You're Marie now. Your life is far too exciting to sit around all day watching the stupid box."

An hour at the airport, an almost four-hour flight and an hour and a half getting to the hotel and checked in was cause for a shower. Dakota kicked off her loafers with a two-inch rubber heel, stripped her casual khakis off, her three-quarter length yellow cotton blouse, and under-clothes, then went into the bathroom. She admired the granite countertops, tile flooring and a walk-in shower. She went over to the shower and started the water. Thank God the toiletries provided were that of the hotel's on-site luxurious spa. At least Dakota didn't have to use bar soap until she could hit the mall.

After lathering up and washing off hours of travel, she stepped out of the shower onto the thick, soft mat and grabbed the thick, soft hotel towel. After drying off, reality hit Dakota. The only clothing she had to put on was the clothing she'd just taken off. Billie, before driving Dakota to the airport, had sat and watched like a hawk as Dakota packed. She made sure she didn't pack anything other than deodorant, a toothbrush and toothpaste.

"Old or new breath; it's still going to stank," Billie had playfully told Dakota.

Even though Dakota had to slip back in the clothes she'd been in all day, she still felt clean. She grabbed her purse then went and got on the elevator, taking it down to the lobby. She took in all the excitement of the casino. With dim overhead lighting, the whole place looked like a disco, lights everywhere. There were scantily dressed cocktail waitresses offering free drinks for those partak-ing in the gambling fun.

Dakota coughed. And there was smoke. She waved her hand across her face. Both she and Marie would have to get used to the smoke. Dakota made her way over to the check-in counter. The line wasn't nearly as long as it was when she arrived to check in, but it was still long nonetheless. She spotted a podium that had a concierge or bell boy behind it. There was only one person in that line and they were already being tended to. She walked over and waited patiently, speaking to a couple of people along the way.

Everyone was just so friendly there, Dakota felt, compared to the folks she ran into every day in Flint. But then again why wouldn't they be? Most people were probably in Vegas on vacation with the big hopes of hitting it big in the casinos. On top of that, drinks were on the house? What wasn't there to be happy about?

"May I help you?" the gentleman behind the podium asked Dakota.

"Yes, sir, you can. I need to do a little shopping." She paused. "Well, actually a lot, but just a little for now. Where is a great place to shop?"

"Well, it depends on your taste. A lot of the hotels on the strip have some amazing shops, including right here at the Rio. There are the Forum Shops at Caesars located inside Caesars Palace hotel, but they are pretty high end. Then you have the discount shops such as Ross along the strip and the Fashion Show Mall on the strip. With 1,888,151 square feet of space, it's one of the largest enclosed malls in the world.

"Oooohh. A Ross." Dakota was always on a budget and loved stores such as Ross, TJ Maxx, and Marshalls. That was music to her ears.

"Yes, ma'am, and our complimentary shuttle can . . ."

While the gentleman spoke to Dakota, so did Marie. Marie wanted to go to the Forum Shops at Caesars. It sounded so elegant, and it was definitely something new. Dakota had to agree with her inner voice. Perhaps Dakota might have loved discount shops, but Marie wanted to ball like Tasha Mack from the BET sitcom *The Game*. No one could predict to the day how much time they had on this earth. What if she never made it back to Vegas again in her life? Then she'd never be able to say she hit the high-end shops at Caesars Palace Las Vegas.

You only live once.

"The Forum Shops. I'd like to go there," Dakota told the gentleman, interrupting his spiel.

He then gave her instructions on how to go about taking the free shuttle over to the strip. He also provided her a map of the strip, circling Caesars Palace for her.

"Thank you, sir."

"Enjoy, ma'am."

Dakota made her way outside the hotel to wait on the shuttle. While waiting, she saw limos picking up and dropping off people as well as Town Cars. The last time she rode in a limo was prom. As she stared at the limo she pondered whether to go for it. She'd only been in Vegas an hour; she'd rather spend that kind of money on shoes versus a ten-minute limo ride.

"You should go for it," she heard a female voice say behind her.

Dakota turned to see a tall, blond-haired woman who looked like she'd just finished up a fashion shoot.

"I see you looking at those limos like a hungry lioness seeking out her next meal."

Dakota smirked. "I wouldn't say all that, but, yeah, limo versus free shuttle. It's a no-brainer." Dakota didn't want to just throw money away. That wasn't being boring or not taking a risk. In her opinion, that was being wise.

"Exactly, it is a no-brainer, so why are you standing here contemplating? They really aren't that expensive. But then again, I guess any ride in life can cost you more than you bargained for depending on where you're heading."

"Oh, well, I'm just heading over to Caesars to do a little shopping," Dakota said.

"The Forum Shops. I love it! There's Louis Vuitton, Christian Louboutin, Fendi, Gucci, Michael Kors, Tiffany & Company, Valentino. It's orgasmic for someone like myself!"

The woman's European accent didn't go unnoticed by Dakota. Perhaps this woman was some famous model from France or someplace.

"I've never been." And hearing the woman call off all those high-priced designer stores, she wasn't sure if she wanted to go; maybe to window shop, but not make a purchase. "The concierge inside suggested it."

"He has good taste." The woman eyeballed Dakota. "And obviously so do you."

"Well thank you." *Oh, my God, did I just blush? What the . . .*

"Are you a Vegas virgin?"

"Excuse me?" Dakota didn't see that one coming.

"Is this your first time in Vegas is all I meant," the woman cleared up. "I didn't mean to offend you."

"Oh, yes. This is my first time in Vegas," Dakota said. "And not to worry." She paused and gave the woman a once-over, noticing her long, slender, tanned legs sticking out from under her short dress. "I don't offend easily." *Did I just look this woman up and down?*

Yes, indeed Dakota had. She had admired all five feet and ten inches of this well-endowed bombshell. Had she done it in a sister girlfriend way? Or, had she done it in a "this woman is hot" way? It didn't matter. The free shuttle was pulling up, putting an end to whatever it was going on between Dakota and the woman before it could even get started.

"Well, here's my ride." Dakota smiled.

"So you're not going to go for it, huh?" The woman tsked and then shook her head. "Too bad. You only live once."

Dakota stopped and looked at the woman. It was as if the woman had just said the secret password. Like Dakota was on some 007 mission and her allies were given the secret code so she'd know who to trust.

"Trust me, you should take the limo," the woman said. "As a matter of fact, if you want company, I'd love to join you. The Forum Shops are like my second home here in Vegas."

"Really?"

"Yes. I dress people. High-profile people. They like quality." The woman looked Dakota up and down again. "I like quality. And since I do this for a living, just look at it as a freebie from me."

"So you'll dress me for free?"

"Certainly," the woman said. She then leaned into Dakota, her glossy lips barely brushing against Dakota's ear. "And undress you as well if you'd prefer."

This wasn't the first time Dakota's private had tingled, but it was the first time a woman's touch, or barely touch, had made it tingle. This whole alter ego thing was going to a whole other level. Perhaps Dakota was getting lost in it all.

"So what do you say . . ." The woman searched for a name to call Dakota, placing a hand on Dakota's shoulder.

"Marie," Dakota said, almost mesmerized by the woman's touch, by the woman's eyes gazing into hers.

"What do you say, Marie?"

Trying not to pant and to get her heart palpitations under control, Dakota replied with, "I say yes."

On that note the woman signaled down one of the limo drivers who had just been standing against his car. "Are you available?" she asked the driver.

He looked at his watch. "I have a client coming out in about an hour."

"I just need you long enough to take us over to Caesars hotel."

The driver thought for a moment.

"Come on. You'll be back in less than a half hour for sure."

"Ahhh, all right." The driver then walked around and opened the door for Dakota and the woman to get in.

"After you," the woman said to Dakota.

"Thank you." Dakota went to get inside the car. Right before getting in she stopped and then turned to the woman. "Wait. I don't even know your name."

"How rude of me. It's Aquilla. Aquilla Humphrey."

Dakota smiled. "Nice to meet you, Aquilla. And thanks for the ride." Dakota got in the limo and Aquilla slid in after her.

"Giving you a ride is my pleasure, dear," Aquilla said and then the driver closed the door. "Hopefully it will be considered one of the best rides of your life." With that, Aquilla rested her hand on Dakota's knee and they drove off.

Chapter 5

When the two women stepped out of the limo, Aquilla handed the driver a hundred dollar bill and then escorted Dakota into the Caesars Palace hotel. Dakota found this hotel to be beautiful as well. It didn't have that posh, groovy feel like the Rio, but it was very elegant indeed, classy even. It looked like money. Smelled like money. If Dakota ever did make it back to Vegas, she was going to give Caesars Palace a try for sure.

"Thank you so much for the limo ride, Aquilla," Dakota said. "I'll take care of it on the way back."

"No worries," Aquilla said. "This is where I'm staying. I was just at the Rio doing an emergency dress for one of my peers. My real client who flew me here is actually staying here."

"Oh, okay."

"Do I hear a hint of disappointment in your voice that you'll be riding back solo?" Aquilla asked, placing her index finger on Dakota's chin and just slightly lifting it up.

"Ummm, perhaps." Dakota pouted her lips. "You were pretty good company."

"Well, don't be sad, dear, let's take advantage of the time we have now. So let's go shopping."

After taking a set of escalators up to the shops, Dakota was in awe. The shops were absolutely exquisite. It didn't take her long to realize that she should have gone with her first instincts and hit Ross. She was way out of her league here. If she bought one outfit in this place, more than likely she'd have to wear it her entire Vegas trip because it would exhaust her budget.

"I know the perfect shop for you." Aquilla grabbed Dakota by the hand and took her into a shop in which every outfit the mannequins had on looked like something someone more of Aquilla's shape and size would look good in rather than Dakota.

"Uh, I don't know." Dakota began to fidget.

"What? Not your taste? Too risqué for you?" Aquilla fondled the red sequin dress that one of the mannequins was wearing.

"Oh, no. Everything looks absolutely beautiful." Dakota looked around. "Everything in here is beautiful. You have amazing taste indeed to bring me here. It's my taste I suppose. Or should I say my size? I don't think I can fit into the dressing room, let alone the clothes."

"Nonsense!" Aquilla spat. "You are perfect for anything in here. Come." Aquilla once again grabbed Dakota by the hand. This time she led her over to the dressing room mirror. "Look at that. Do you know how many women I dress would pay for these curves?" She laughed. "Screw that. Do you know how many women I have dressed who have paid for these curves? What are you, a size sixteen?" Aquilla began to run her hands down Dakota's sides. She paused. "Do you mind?"

All Dakota could do was shake her head in the negative. So Aquilla continued.

I bet if she were a man her dick would be hard right about now, Dakota thought, and then chuckled. *Hell I ain't a man and my dick is hard.* Dakota chuckled even louder at the foul-mouthed voice within.

"What's wrong?" Aquilla asked her giggling new friend.

"Oh, nothing. I'm sorry. It just tickled a little, that's all." Dakota straightened up and got serious.

"I'm very serious here. You are a beautiful woman. I'm sure you might hear that all the time, but do you believe it?" She turned Dakota to face her. Staring into Dakota's eyes she repeated, "Well, do you believe it? That you are a beautiful woman?"

All Dakota could see was Aquilla's pearly pink glossed lips staring back at her. Waiting. Waiting for her answer or waiting to be kissed? Dakota wasn't sure which. Those lips appeared to be getting closer and closer to Dakota, the longer she stared. But was she the one moving in, or was it Aquilla moving in close to her? All she knew is that she could practically count every little piece of shining glitter in that lip gloss. Dakota felt her own lips parting and before she knew it, she was being sharply turned back toward the mirror.

"Well." Aquilla waited. "Do you?"

"I do," Dakota said, almost in a trance. She then repeated, "I do," with much more confidence, lifting her shoulders up.

"Now that's more like it. There is nothing worse than dressing a client with low self-esteem and doubt, too afraid and ashamed of their figure to even try on garments that were absolutely made for them." She threw her hands up and clapped. She then turned Dakota back to face her. "My, oh my, am I going to have fun with you."

Dakota felt like Aquilla's little Baby Alive doll that she was about to play dress-up with, especially since she kept grabbing her hand and dragging her around the store like she was her favorite dolly.

Aquilla had summoned clerk after clerk to assist them with different styles and sizes. In an hour's time, Dakota had dang near tried on everything in the store.

"Perfect!" Aquilla gasped when Dakota came out of the dressing room wearing a sleek black dress. It hung just right off the shoulders; not too much. It was about two inches above the knee, showing off what Aquilla referred to as Dakota's delicious knees. "And I know where to grab you the perfect pair of shoes." Aquilla looked at the clerk. "We'll take it!"

"Whoa, whoa." Dakota held her hand up and then searched for the tag. Although she'd had a ball playing dress-up, after trying on a pair of pants that cost $495, she knew she wouldn't even be buying a pair of socks out of that joint. She didn't even want to embarrass herself by looking at the price tag on a whole dress, but she was about to do just that. Having her credit card declined would be even more embarrassing she surmised.

Aquilla put her hand right back up. She closed her eyes and started shaking her head. "No, no, no. I will not take no for an answer. You must let me purchase this dress for you. My friend, I have been dressing people for years and it's very rare to come across a garment that was specifically made for that person. Darling, no one, and I mean no one, can wear this dress the way you are wearing it. Don't do this to me. You'll totally bruise my ego." She walked close to Dakota and lifted Dakota's dark, shoulder-length hair that was a mixture of kinks and waves. "If you turn me down, I don't think I'll ever be able to dress another woman the same."

Was Aquilla this darn sensual or was Dakota hearing things? Seeing things. Her voice purred like an arching kitten. Her lips were like luscious pretty pink cotton candy that spoke only sweet words.

"But I—"

Dakota started to speak but was silenced by Aquilla's soft index finger. Dakota could only imagine what else Aquilla could do with that finger as that damn tingling shit started again.

"Shhh. Please. How often in your lifetime will a complete stranger meet you and just want to buy you a thousand dollar dress with nothing in return. No strings attached?"

Dakota couldn't give Aquilla an honest number of times that could happen. Well, an honest number was probably zero. Once upon a time Dakota recalled her churchgoing auntie saying that God can put it in people's spirit to bless complete strangers with a house and a car if He saw fit. For some reason, Dakota didn't think God had anything to do with this, but still, in the words of her auntie, she wasn't about to pass up this blessing.

"You are right. I seriously doubt if a perfect stranger will ever buy me something this nice." Dakota turned to look in the mirror and admired herself in the dress one more time. She had to admit, Aquilla knew her stuff. It did look as though this dress had been made for her figure. A size eight couldn't do what her size eighteen was doing for this dress; no way, no how. "And you're right about something else, too. I do look good in this dress. It was made for me indeed." Dakota ran her hands down her sides as Aquilla had done earlier. She closed her eyes and enjoyed her own touch.

"Not here, darling," Aquilla whispered in her ear. "Later, when you're back in your hotel room in the shower, save it for then. And imagine my hands instead of yours."

Dakota opened her eyes. She was looking into Aquilla's eyes through the mirror. "But you said no strings attached."

"I just said to imagine it is all." Aquilla winked and began to walk away.

The clerk who had been assisting them stopped her. "So does she want that dress?"

"Yes, she's taking the size sixteen," Aquilla replied.

Dakota poked her head through the dressing room door, as she'd already walked back inside to take the dress off. "No. Eighteen. I wear size eighteen."

"Perhaps," Aquilla said, "but you look better in a sixteen. Take a look at the tag."

Dakota lifted her left arm and grabbed hold of the tag underneath with her right arm. "What?"

Aquilla smiled. "Mostly everything you've been trying on has been a sixteen," Aquilla said proudly. "The minute you said you wore a size eighteen I immediately knew that was incorrect. I'd sized you up the entire ride over here. And I know a woman's body. It's my job to know," she expressed. "You wear a size eighteen because that's what you feel most comfortable in. Darling, life is not about being comfortable. Life is about looking fabulous." Aquilla looked to the clerk. "Like I said, she'll take the size sixteen." Then she walked off not sticking around to take any lip from Dakota. Before she left Dakota's earshot, though, she threw over her shoulder, "Disrobe, darling, so you can ring out. We still have a pair of killer pumps to get to go with the ensemble."

Dakota went into the dressing room and changed out of the dress. The clerk was waiting at the door to take it and go ring it up. By the time Dakota put her clothes back on and came out of the dressing room, the dress had been rung up, paid for, and was bagged. Aquilla stood at the exit door waiting for Dakota with bag in hand.

"All set?" Aquilla asked, extending the bag to Dakota.

"All set." Dakota took the bag from Aquilla.

The two women exited the store hand in hand. Only this time Aquilla didn't have to snatch up Dakota's hand and drag her along. Dakota took the liberty of placing it inside Aquilla's.

They entered a shoe store where the shoes weren't too pricey, at least not for the quality anyway. Dakota looked around, but Aquilla appeared to have known just the right shoe to set the dress off. Dakota didn't even have to try on a million pair.

Dakota watched as Aquilla instructed the clerk to bring out two different pair of shoes. She'd called them out by name without even having gone to search the shoe rack.

"In black," Aquilla had told the clerk.

"What size?" the clerk asked.

"Hmmm." Aquilla turned and looked at Dakota's feet.

"Oh, I wear—" Dakota started once she noticed the clerk and Aquilla looking at her feet.

"Seven," Aquilla said to the clerk.

"Yes, ma'am," the clerk said, then scurried off into the back where the shoes were stored.

"How did you . . ." Dakota didn't even finish her query. She'd answered herself by resolving that it was Aquilla's job to know.

A couple minutes later the clerk appeared with two very similar looking shoes. She slipped a stocking on Dakota's foot and slipped one of the shoes on her foot.

"I love it!" Dakota said.

"That was my first choice," Aquilla said, clapping her hands again in excitement. She looked to the clerk. "You can put the other pair back."

The clerk nodded and did just that.

Dakota slipped on the other shoe. She then stood up, walked over to the mirror, and modeled the shoes, turning her feet this way and that way. "What a simple yet gorgeous shoe. I will not argue with you about taking these."

Aquilla cleared her throat as if she had a problem.

"What is it?" Dakota asked confused. She turned and looked at Aquilla.

"The dress was on me. The shoes are on you," Aquilla said.

"Oh, I'm sorry. I didn't mean it like that," Dakota apologized. "I meant that I won't argue with you about them being perfect for me, therefore me buying them. I hope you don't think I'm that kind of girl because—"

"Ahh, enough." Aquilla walked over to Dakota. For the second time Aquilla placed her index finger on Dakota's lips.

Internally Dakota vowed that if that pretty little finger touched her lips again, she would suck it like a lollypop.

"It's fine. Relax. I know you are not that kind of girl." Aquilla's eyes rolled over Dakota's body nice and slow. "That's what I like about you." She slowly dragged her finger down Dakota's lips.

By the time the tip of her index finger reached the opening of Dakota's lips, Dakota had indiscreetly, but purposely, stuck out the tip of her tongue, capturing just a bit of Aquilla's fingertip.

Aquilla smiled, puckered her lips and shook her head, all while wagging her finger in Dakota's face. "Please don't. You're going to defeat the purpose of me not buying the shoes for you."

"Huh? I don't get it," Dakota said. "Ohhh. I get it. The old superstition. If you buy someone a pair of shoes they are going to walk all over you with them."

"No, I'm not superstitious at all."

"Then what it is?"

"Plain and simple. I've bought you a dress with no strings attached," Aquilla said. "If I buy shoes, then I get to fuck you." And on that note, Aquilla walked away just as the clerk came out of the back.

With tomato red cheeks, Dakota began to scoop up the shoes to carry them over to the counter. Ringing up just under $150, Dakota didn't feel like she'd done too much damage. Basically she'd gotten an entire outfit for the night for $150 since she didn't have to pay for the dress. She was definitely still within budget.

With her bags in hand, Dakota met Aquilla over at the door to exit.

"Well, my love, looks like you are all set with the perfect outfit. I hope you wear it someplace special."

"Well, actually, I have a reception to attend this evening. It will be perfect."

"More than perfect, with you in it." Aquilla rubbed Dakota's cheek. There were a couple moments of silence.

"Well, I have to see about my client shortly. I should go."

"Well, thank you so much, Aquilla, for everything. This was truly a first . . . for more than you will ever know."

"I'm sure. It's been my pleasure. I like providing people with a first lifetime experience." Aquilla opened the little snazzy clutch she'd been carrying and pulled out her business card. She handed it to Dakota.

Dakota looked at the card. "Italy? You're from Italy?"

"That's where I call home, but I'm here in the States far more than I am home. I have a place in New York and my clients in L.A. usually put me up at some really nice spots. If you're ever in either area, look me up." Aquilla wrapped her hands around Dakota's hand that held the card. "I'd love to be your first at other things."

Dakota smiled as Aquilla released her hand and began to walk away. And Dakota couldn't stop watching her. Dakota was sad to watch her walk away. This was the most carefree, unbelievable, spur-of-the-moment thing Dakota had ever experienced and she owed it all to Aquilla. As if being lured to Aquilla, like a magnet, Dakota followed her. Feeling as though she was being followed, Aquilla turned on her heels to run dead smack into Dakota. She opened her mouth to speak, which was a golden opportunity for Dakota.

Without even thinking about it so that she wouldn't change her mind, Dakota allowed her mouth to meet Aquilla's. The two women's tongues danced in each other's mouths like the kiss had been choreographed. The electric volt that ran between the women kept their eyes open. They stared into each other's eyes like long-time lovers and allowed their eyes and tongues to do all the talking.

When the kiss ended, Dakota was out of breath and her lower face was covered with pink, pearly, glittery lip gloss. Slowly, Dakota backed up until she knew she was close to the escalator. She looked over her shoulder to make sure she was getting on it safely, then turned to look at Aquilla one last time. No words were spoken between the two as Dakota went down the escalator, Aquilla disappearing from her sight.

Catching her breath, Dakota made her way through the hotel and out the exit door where several cabs were lined up for waiting passengers. After just a minute or two, Dakota was up next.

"Where to?" the doorman asked Dakota so that he could relay her destination to the taxi driver.

"The Rio," Dakota replied.

The doorman informed the taxi driver of where he was to take the passenger, then opened the door for Dakota to climb in.

"Thank you," Dakota said, digging in her purse for a couple of one dollar bills to tip the doorman. "Here you go." She handed them to the man.

"Thank you, ma'am," he said with a wave.

"You're welcome," Dakota said as she got into the back of the taxi. "Oh wait."

The doorman stopped right before he was about to close the door. "Yes."

"Could you discard this for me please?" Dakota handed him Aquilla's business card.

"No problem." He took the card.

"Thank you." Dakota got settled into the back seat of the taxi as the driver pulled off. There was no point in Dakota keeping Aquilla's business card. She'd kissed a girl and she liked it. And that was that.

Chapter 6

"Damn New Orleans having voodoo and roots on people and stuff. This Vegas is no joke," Dakota said as she scurried through the casino heading toward the elevator bank. Shyla had called her just as she was entering the hotel.

"Well they don't call it Sin City for nothing, girlie," Shyla said through the phone receiver. "So I take from that comment that in just the little bit of time you've been there you've managed to get into a little trouble." Shyla laughed. "Who am I kidding? This is Dakota I'm talking to. Not even Vegas can change a person overnight. And it hasn't even been a night."

"Well . . ." Dakota started. She was planning on telling Shyla all about her encounter with Leon and her rendezvous with Aquilla, but Shyla would never believe it in a million years. Dakota herself half believed it. Why even bother wasting her breath? Besides, this side of her wasn't something she expected to keep up anyway. Here in Vegas no one knew her. Back home girls who did some of the things she'd already done or might do would surely gain a reputation. Dakota's reputation was good back in the city and she wanted to keep it that way.

"Anyway," Shyla said, "I just want you to have fun, your kind of fun. I just want you to be happy and do what makes you comfortable. Who cares if you flew all the way to Vegas to curl up under the TV?" Shyla said. "You're a good girl, Dakota. I know we give you mad grief about it, but there's nothing wrong with it. You just keep doing you."

Shyla's words made Dakota smile. She loved her friend and how her friend would take her however she came. But in just the few hours Dakota had decided to open up, the world had opened right back up for her. She wanted more.

"I'll keep doing me," Dakota said. "You definitely don't have to worry about that."

"All right then. I love you, girl."

"Love you too," Dakota said before ending the call.

Although Shyla's parting words had touched her heart, they, at the same time, saddened her. Had she really been that big of a bore all her life? Evidently, she had. She couldn't even come up with five good, exciting, fun things she'd done when Billie had inquired. It really shouldn't have taken a trip all the way to the West Coast to force her to have a little fun in her life. But it had. *Better late than never.* And, as the elevator doors parted and about five college hunks now stood before her, Dakota was glad about the timing of it all.

The delicious-looking hunks filed off the elevator; one was even so kind as to hold the elevator door for Dakota.

"Thank you," she said, then tiptoed past him.

"Anytime." He looked her in the eyes. "Which floor?" He was going to go one step further and even push the button for Dakota before he went on about his business.

"Damn, son, why you acting thirsty?" one of his boys shouted from behind him.

"Yeah, she cute and all, but damn. Bring your ass on," another said.

The helpful coed looked torn. Dakota decided to let him off the hook. "That's okay. I've got it. You run along with the fellas and have fun."

"Yeah. But something tells me I could have much more fun on this elevator ride with you."

"I guess you'll never know," Dakota said as the doors closed between them. "Oh, my gosh!" she said out loud, blushing and acting like a schoolgirl herself. She couldn't believe she was instigating and receiving this much attention. Who knew?

Once the elevator deposited her on the eleventh floor, Dakota went to her room. It was a quarter to five. She had just enough time to get herself together for the reception. Since she'd already showered, she opted for a ho bath, even though nothing about her actions from the day made her feel like a ho. She just didn't feel the need to have to douse her entire body with water again. For the second time that day she stripped out of her clothes. Just as she was headed to the shower her cell phone rang.

"Hello," she answered. She didn't spare the two seconds it would have taken to look at the caller ID because she didn't have the two seconds to spare.

"Sister, how's it going? Where are you? You better not be in your hotel room watching television."

"Oh, ye of little faith," Dakota said to Billie. "It's going good actually."

"Hmmm. Not sure if your definition of good is the same as mine."

Dakota sighed and sat down on the bed. "I hate to admit it, but you were right."

"So you have just been sitting in that stupid hotel room watching television. And here I was hoping I hadn't heard from you because you were out doing something you'd never think of doing, or at least shopping. Damn, girl, did my little spiel not infiltrate any part of your being?"

"That's what you were right about. It wasn't until I got here and really decided to just open my mind to new things did I realize that my life has been nothing to write about it. You, Shyla, Trice; you all are so fun. That's why I love being around you guys. I'm nothing like you guys though. I'm really not sure why you guys even want to hang out with me. I'm like Debbie Downer compared to you three." Dakota took a second break before saying, "Sis, if I ask you something, will you be completely honest with me?"

"Aren't I always?"

Dakota rolled her eyes in her head. "Sometimes brutally."

"So shoot."

"I know you give me the time of day because I'm your sister and you pretty much have to by default. But do you think maybe with Shyla and Trice . . ." Dakota had to find the right words. "You know how some people only hang with certain people because they think it makes them look better?"

"Stop it right there," Billie said. "I'm not even going to allow you to insult Shyla and Trice like that. You know as well as I do that they are genuine, good people. They have your back. They've never done anything to prove otherwise."

"Yeah, you're right." Dakota sighed.

"I know I'm right. They've met auntie haven't they? And you know she claims to have that spirit of discernment or whatever it is. She wasted no time telling a couple of my boyfriends that they were the devil or kin to him. So you can best believe she would have called out Laverne and Shirley by now."

Both girls started laughing.

"Why are you crazy?" Dakota asked her sister.

"Because one of us has to be. Now why don't you try being crazy? Forget about what people would think or say. Nobody cares. Go down to the casino, find a complete stranger, and have sex with him in the elevator."

"Hey, I'm in a different state, not country. I have my limits you know."

"Yes, I know, and make the sky your limit."

"The sky's my limit, huh?" Dakota repeated.

"Yes, now fly away, little birdie. Fly away."

"Oh, I hate you."

"Yes, that's because you love me so much and you know I'm right."

"Yeah, yeah, yeah. Look, sis, I have to get ready to go. I've wasted enough time listening to your nonsense. If I didn't know any better, I might think you were setting me up to come here to Las Vegas, do the unthinkable, and then run home to tell you everything so that you can live vicariously through me."

"Yeah, or masturbate while you tell me if it's really good."

"Disgusting! Bye, Billie."

"Love you too. Deuces."

Dakota ended the call and just shook her head. She and Billie were cut from the same cloth indeed, but definitely different corners of the quilt.

Dakota hopped up and headed to the bathroom. She did her wash up and proceeded to get dressed. That's when she realized she'd forgotten to purchase something very important: panties. Now the bra she wouldn't mind wearing again, but she was not going to slip on those drawers her cat had been meowing in all day. No way no how. She'd just have to do something she'd never done before in her life: wear a dress without panties.

As Dakota slipped on the dress, she realized her bra wasn't going to work either, not with the dress being somewhat off the shoulders. Having her bra straps show just looked tacky. And no way did she want the straps of a fourteen dollar bra from Walmart peeking underneath a thousand dollar dress. So both braless and panty-less it would have to be. She could only hope the lighting was dim in the room where the reception was being held.

Dakota washed her face with the facial soap the hotel provided. She made a mental note to visit the cosmetic department at one of the stores in the mall. She'd never given those pesky women always trying to squirt her with cologne or get her to get a makeover or facial the time of day, but Marie would gladly do the honors.

Dakota loved her kinky locks and the fact that all she had to do was wet them, run the comb through them, then scrunch them up with her fingers. Billie always complained about the natural, curly kinks.

"If you'd inherited my long, straight hair," their mother had told Billie once, "you'd be complaining about that. People with curly hair want it straight. People with straight hair want it curly. Just be glad with what the good Lord gave you."

Dakota had always been just that: pleased with all that God had blessed her with. But maybe she'd been too complacent in life. Perhaps accepting everything was the reason she never wanted to do or try anything different. Talk about a gift and a curse.

Blessed with great, clear skin after spending all four years of high school fighting teenage acne, Dakota didn't wear makeup, so she didn't have to worry about fighting with her sister to allow her to bring any.

Fortunately for her, Billie hadn't noticed she was wearing the same single-carat diamond stud earrings that she always wore: a gift from her parents on her twenty-fifth birthday. So at least she had something in her ears.

"All set," she said, looking at herself in the mirror and pulling her dress down. She'd always been fine with her A-cup breasts. Now that she had to go braless via accident, she was even finer that she didn't have to worry about some huge jugs jiggling around. She cupped her small breasts, lifted the left and then the right, then patted her dress down one last time.

She exited the bathroom and went to slip on her shoes. Grabbing her purse, the black one her sister suggested she carry because it would go with everything until she could purchase another one, she exited the room. She walked to the elevators and pushed the down button. Once it arrived, there were a few people dressed in business-casual on the elevator.

"Good evening," Dakota greeted them all like she knew them. A couple replied; another nodded.

While the elevator went down, Dakota took note of the sign in the elevator listing different amenities and guest services of the hotel. She remember that the Rio had a couple shops of their own. On a whim, she pushed the button that led her to the shops. It wasn't anything compared to the Forum Shops. It was, though, nice and elegant and had just what she'd had in mind of purchasing when deciding to go to the shops.

She looked through the glass windows of one of the stores and then entered.

"Hi," the lady running the store said to her.

"Hello. How are you?"

"Just fine. Thank you. Can I help you find anything in particular?"

"As a matter of fact you can. I see you have cosmetics." Dakota pointed and then began walking toward the counter that cased cosmetics.

"Yes, we do, and a nice little selection at that. Don't tell me: you forgot to pack your makeup case." The woman shooed her hand and chuckled. "Happens all the time. I'm sure we have some shades and colors that will work well with your skin tone." The clerk began to fiddle with some of the products. "What colors do you usually wear?" She began holding up different products next to Dakota's skin.

"Red. Red lipstick. I'd like a tube of red lipstick." Dakota didn't hesitate as she scanned the lipstick selections. "That one right there."

"Well, that's a gloss."

"I want it," Dakota said.

"Then you've got it. Anything else?"

Dakota did one last once-over of the makeup selection. "No, just the red lipstick. I mean lip gloss."

"All right." The woman grabbed Dakota's selection and then walked over to the cash register.

Dakota looked around the store as the clerk began to bag the lipstick. That's when she noticed some ruby red teardrop earrings. "And these!" She quickly snatched the earrings off the spinning jewelry stand and walked them over to the clerk.

"Lovely!" She looked Dakota up and down. "You are going to be the belle of the ball for sure. Simple but so elegant indeed. Not too much but more than enough." She winked. "And this red is just enough garnish so as not to take away from the main dish." She smiled.

Dakota returned the smile.

The clerk packaged Dakota's items and then rang them up. "$59.73. Would that be cash, credit, or if you are staying here at the hotel, charged to your room?"

"I am staying here. Can I have that charged to my room please?"

"Certainly. I just need to see your card."

Dakota pulled out her room key and handed it to the clerk.

"No, the hotel card; the one they gave you at check in for—"

"Oh, yes." Dakota thumped herself upside the head. "I'm sorry. Forgive me. It's been a long day." Dakota pulled out the card the check-in desk had explained to her was connected to the credit card she'd left on file for any incidentals or hotel charges.

"I completely understand." The clerk waited patiently until Dakota handed her the proper card. "Thank you." After charging the items to Dakota's room, she handed the card back as well as her items. "Thank you so much. Come back if you need anything else."

"Will do," Dakota replied and then exited the store. Next she found the ladies' room. She went inside and headed straight for the mirror. She removed the studs from her ears and placed them in the zippered change compartment of her purse. Next she took the newly purchased ones and placed them into her pierced ears. She shifted her head from side to side admiring them while thinking, *I hope the clerk was right; that this isn't too much. Especially, for a business function.*

Next Dakota took out her tube of lip gloss and dressed her lips in it. She stared at her lips through the mirror and couldn't help but think about Aquilla's pink ones, the ones on her face. Doing so caused her to, this time, quiver. No tingle, at least, just a quiver.

She placed the lip gloss in her purse and threw the bag away. She was now ready to go register for her conference. She backed away from the mirror and looked at herself. She twisted her lips in thought. She opened her purse and dug around for the hair twisty she always kept in her purse for whenever she just wanted to get her hair off her neck. Usually she'd just slap her hair in a messy ponytail, but this time she wanted her locks to sit atop her head.

Putting the twisty around her wrist, she went to the sink, wet her hands, and then pulled her hair up on top of her head. She pulled out a couple of deliberate stray stands and her new five-second hairstyle was complete.

"Yes," she said with satisfaction. As she looked at herself in the mirror with her updo, a style she never wore her hair in, and her red lip gloss, a shade she had never dared to wear, she hardly recognized herself. Which was the point.

Wiggling her hips in the dress Aquilla had convinced her was made just for her figure, she had to 100 percent, wholeheartedly agree. She winked at herself and was on her merry way.

Within minutes she was in the lobby where registration and the reception were taking place. After exiting the elevator that had brought her to her final destination, she had spotted the long registration table. It felt like a mile away amidst all the chattering insurance industry folks, who were 95 percent men. They were all mingling, networking, drinking, and socializing. Dakota felt like a minnow in a shark tank, but she shook that feeling off. The Dakota who would have coward up, been invisible as she made her way over to the registration table, registered, and then gone back to her room for the night, was hundreds of miles away. The new and improved Dakota looked too damn good and had spent $200 to look that good, although the total package was valued at $1,200. But if you included the body up under all the accessories—*priceless!* So she wasn't about to hide up under her shell.

Dakota sashayed over to the registration table, greeting anyone her eyes locked with along the way. She'd never realized how confident looking someone in the eyes made a person feel. How confident it made her look to others. People were looking at her like she was a boss chick. Like she had it going on. She could see the vote of confidence in their eyes. People were rooting for her and she had no idea why. Was this how people had always looked at her, or was it the dress, four-inch pumps that literally pushed her up to another level, the earrings, or red lip gloss? She had no idea because she'd never paid attention. Well, now she was. And what she really liked was that others were paying attention too—to her.

Chapter 7

"I'm sorry. I don't see a Marie Smith on the registration list," said the female handling registration for participants whose last names ended in S through Z. "I see an Amy Smith, Dakota Smith, a—"

"That's me. Dakota Marie Smith." Dakota smiled away her embarrassment. She was taking this Marie thing too far. Sure it was her middle name, but the only time anyone ever used it was when they were scolding or trying to let her know they meant business. Here in Vegas she'd taken the edge off of the name. But standing there at the registration desk was just a reminder of who she really was, and not to get too comfortable with this whole alter ego thing.

"Oh, okay, you're Dakota," the clerk said with raised eyebrows.

"Sorry. All my friends and family call me Marie. I'm so used to going by Marie. I forget who I really am sometimes." That wasn't totally true. But the plan was to at least forget while she was in Vegas.

"No problem." The registration clerk had found truth in Dakota's lies. She began gathering a folder, papers, notebook, and pen. She placed it all in a nice tote bag that was branded with the name of the conference on the front and the sponsors on the back. "Here you go, Ms. Smith." She handed Dakota the bag. "And just one second while I get your nametag." The woman eyeballed the rows of alphabetically placed name badges in sturdy clear plastic attached to a lanyard. "And here you go," she said once she came across Dakota's. She extended it to her.

"Thank you." Dakota took the badge and placed it inside her tote instead of placing it around her neck. She'd save doing that for during the actual sessions. Right now, she had a thousand dollar dress she needed to show off and she didn't want some eyesore of a badge to take anything away from it.

There was a slight chill in the room. The temperature at most conferences was usually freezing cold. The fact that this one was in a desert state only gave them more of a reason to keep a chill going. Dakota tried to discretely look down to make sure her hardened nipples weren't poking through the material of her dress. She was safe. Feeling comfortable, she made her way over to the open bar that was serving cocktails.

"And what can I get you?" the bartender asked.

Dakota looked to the man standing next to her who had already been waiting when she walked up. She looked back to the bartender. "I think this gentleman was next."

Realizing Dakota was referring to him, the man tore himself from the conversation he was having with another attendee. "Oh, no, I've been taken care of already. Thank you anyway." He then quickly, and not in a creepy way, gave Dakota the once-over. "But even if I hadn't been, ladies first."

Dakota returned the smile he was throwing her way. She then turned to the bartender and ordered an, "Apple martini, please." She had no idea what an apple martini even tasted like. She just remembered the women on one of her favorite shows of all time, *Sex and the City,* ordering them. She'd lived vicariously through those women once upon a time. Well now she was living vicariously through herself.

"One apple martini, coming up!" The bartender took one more order from a man who had walked up on Dakota's other side then went to prepare both drinks. A minute later Dakota was placing a dollar bill in the tip glass on the bar and sipping on her drink as she cased her surroundings.

"Hello. How are you? Good evening." She greeted everyone she made eye contact with.

"Beautiful dress," one of the very few other women there complimented Dakota.

"Thank you. It's new." Dakota back in Flint would have downplayed the compliment and told the woman how she'd had the dress in her closet for years and had just decided to get some wear out of it. Whether that was true or not, she never was one who could just accept an outright compliment. It was like she didn't deserve it or something. But not tonight. She felt worthy of any compliment that came her way.

An hour and two martinis later, Dakota had greeted at least half the people in the room, exchanged names and some light information from others about where they worked and where they were from. Of course there was industry talk as well. For the most part, Dakota was pleased with her little venture. But after two martinis she had one other place to venture off to.

"The ladies' room?" she asked the same woman who had registered her. The woman pointed and Dakota followed her finger with her eyes. "Thank you." She set her empty glass down on one of the tall, skirted tables made for standing only and, with tote bag in hand, made her way to the ladies' room.

After entering the stall and closing the door behind her, she placed the tote, which now contained her purse, on the hook on the back of the door. Next she lifted her dress and went to pull her underwear down, only to find her nails slightly scratching her skin. "Oh snaps." *I'm not wearing any.* Dakota began to laugh like the tipsy chick she was.

She managed to take care of her business, stumbling only once. The alcohol was starting to play with her a little bit. Her tolerance was really low because Dakota was good for babysitting a drink all night: that same one drink, chasing it with a Coke or water. Needless to say, there was never an argument among her and her girls about who the designated driver would be.

She pulled out her cell phone to check the time. It was around 7:00 p.m. The evening was definitely still young Vegas time, but her body was still on Eastern Standard. Besides that, it had been a long day. It was ten o'clock at home. Unless it was Thursday and she had plans to spend the next hour with Olivia Pope and cast, she would be in bed, resting up for work the next day. Even on weekends she'd find herself turning in, leaving the television on only to put her to sleep.

That did not sound like the life of a twenty-five-year-old. Why hadn't she realized that before? Even so, no one could blame her for wanting to tap out this early. She'd been up and at it since the break of dawn.

Putting her phone away, Dakota exited the bathroom and headed for the elevators. She pushed the up button. When it arrived, the doors opened to an older man. He was pushing about seventy in age, but had clearly kept himself in tiptop shape, having the body of a fifty-year-old. His smooth brown skin had few wrinkles. He made a wise decision about coloring the gray in his hair. It was very becoming and attractive on him.

"Good evening," he greeted Dakota as she got on the elevator.

"Evening," Dakota returned. The elevator doors shut in front of her.

"Which floor?" the gentleman asked.

"Eleven please."

He turned and looked at her. "Oh, this one is going down."

"Shoot." Dakota slightly stomped her $150 pump. Well, seventy-five dollar, since it was just half of the pair. She hadn't even paid attention to the up or down arrow when the elevator had arrived. She'd just jumped on. "Oh well. I guess I'll just have to ride it back up." Dakota looked at the elevator keypad and saw that the casino button was lit up. "Going to get your gamble on, I see."

Dakota really wanted to take back and swallow her words. She was talking to this man as if he was some young, hip guy. On top of that, he looked to be from India or something. If he was anything like the students from India Dakota had gone to school with, he was probably brilliant and didn't butcher the English vocabulary in any aspect. Perhaps she was stereotyping; still, she hoped she hadn't appeared like some unprofessional ditz.

"Actually, I am going to go try my luck. See what comes of it," he said. "And you? Do you gamble?"

"Oh, no. I'd rather give it to the homeless than to a machine." She laughed. "Besides, I've heard horror stories about people gambling their lives away."

"Oh, those are people who gamble for something other than fun."

"Fun? There's such a thing as gambling for fun?" Dakota shrugged. "I guess; if you call losing all your money fun, so be it."

"There's penny slots. I would hardly consider losing five hundred pennies putting anybody in the poorhouse."

"Pennies?" Even though the city of Detroit was a neighboring city of Flint and housed the infamous MGM Grand Casino, that just wasn't something that ever interested Dakota. Trice and Shyla loved driving over to Detroit and spending the night gambling. Dakota had always passed. In spite of the girls trying to convince her otherwise, she just couldn't see where withdrawing her money from the ATM and in turn feeding it back into another machine, with no guaranteed return, was fun. And now here this gentleman was even telling her one could feed pennies to the machine. Really?

"Yes. They have penny slots," the man confirmed as the elevator stopped. "You really should try it." The elevator doors opened.

"Nah. I think I'm going to go with my first instincts and turn in for the night."

The man stepped out of the elevator, but turned to continue his conversation with Dakota. "It's far too early for a young girl like yourself to be heading up to her room." The elevator door went to close, but he stuck his hand out to stop the door from closing, then continued to hold it open. "But hey, who am I to judge? You could have your husband up there waiting in your room for you with a bubble bath, wine, and chocolates." He looked down at her hands, mainly her left one. Her ring finger. "Well, do you?"

Dakota smiled and shook her head.

"Then what's stopping you? Come on, you only live once."

Dakota shook her head again.

The man shrugged and tsked. "Oh well. Enjoy your evening." He gave her a salute as the elevator doors closed.

Dakota hit the button and the elevator began its upward climb. The entire ride up there was this voice in her head saying, *I can't believe you are going to let an old man outdo you, have fun in the casino while you go catch some Zs.*

By the time the elevator reached Dakota's floor and the doors opened, she'd had a change of heart. She hit the close door button, next the casino button, then waited as the elevator took her back down to the casino.

Once she exited the elevator, she had that entire Alice in Wonderland thing going on again. Lights flashing, music from the machines, maybe a live band somewhere; Dakota wasn't sure where it was coming from, but she heard music. She heard laughter and screams of excitement. This was a whole new world: one she was willing, ready, and able to conquer.

She slowly walked around like a deer in headlights as she watched people gamble, drink, and smoke. Back in Flint smoking wasn't allowed in public places, and neither was walking around the streets with an open alcohol container either. But in her cab ride back from shopping, she'd seen several people indulging in alcoholic beverages while they walked the strip.

After milling around for a while, Dakota looked up and saw that the area of slot machines she was at had signs that read 1 CENT hanging above them. A gambler she was not, but the old man was right. Losing 500 pennies wasn't anything like losing $500, so she went into her purse and retrieved her wallet. She pulled out a ten dollar bill then found an empty slot machine to sit down and play at.

"Oh, I'm playing that one too," a middle-aged black woman said to Dakota as she went to sit down.

That's when Dakota noticed that the woman's leg was resting on the bar on the bottom of the chair she was about to sit down in. The woman also had some card or something on an old-fashioned telephone cord–looking thing. It was plugged into the slot machine.

"Oh, sorry," Dakota said, then moved on to the next empty penny slot she saw. "Is it okay to sit here?" She decided to ask the person on either side of her this time.

"Oh, no, baby," an older woman said.

The other person was too into whatever it was going on at their machine to offer a verbal reply. He just shook his head with a look on his face that cursed the day Dakota was born for interrupting his love affair with the slot.

Dakota sat down and examined the machine. Once she discovered where she should stick the ten dollar bill she did just that. There were some bells and whistles and then the machine patiently waited for Dakota to place a bet. Not realizing what she'd done, she hit the MAX button. A few objects scattered about on the screen in front of her; then the next thing she knew the machine started singing and there was this voice telling her it was time to do the progressive.

Dakota had no idea what the heck was going on or what to do next, but then the money bags that appeared on the screen made it obvious. She touched one of the bags and it burst open. The number 500 appeared; then there was a pause. She touched another bag, 120 appeared. She touched two more bags and the numbers 1,000 and 300 appeared. The next bag she touched made this wonk wonk sound, there was a splat, and then the number zero. Her machine start doing this repetitive clinking sound as if someone was feeding it coins and the numbers under the CREDIT portion started getting higher and higher. When all was said and done, Dakota had 2,830 credits, which was 1,830 more than she'd started with. After that much excitement, Dakota figured that machine had done all it was going to do to entertain her, so she looked over the machine until she saw a button that read CASH OUT.

She hit that button and heard that same clinking noise, only no coins were falling out of the machine. Instead the machine spit out some slip of paper. She pulled it out and held it up to examine. She discovered that it was a voucher worth twenty-eight dollars and thirty cents.

"Not bad, depending on what you started with."

Startled by the voice, Dakota turned around to see who was taking to her. Her face relaxed when she saw a familiar face. "Oh, hi again."

"I see you decided to come down here and join us lost souls who have decided to gamble our life savings away."

Dakota laughed at the older man's sense of humor. "Yes, I did. You made me feel as though I was missing something. And I didn't want to miss a thing," Dakota replied.

"So . . ." He nodded toward Dakota's voucher. "How much did you start out with?"

"Oh." She put her attention back on the voucher. "Just ten dollars."

"Okay." He nodded his approval. "Then you made a come up."

"Beginner's luck, I'm sure."

"Well, I'm glad for you, this vet is already down more than I care to admit." He thought for a second, snapped his finger, and then said with excitement, "I got it. You're beginner's luck." He grabbed Dakota by the hand. "Come with me."

She couldn't even refuse before the man was dragging her across the casino. What was it with the folks in Vegas dragging her around like she was some rag doll? Eventually Dakota and the man came to a halt at a long table, not long enough to be a pool table though. Several people were gathered around it. Different colored chips sat in front of people as dice rolled.

"Aw, craps," a man who'd just rolled the dice said and snapped. "I'm done." He picked up the few chips in front of him that he had left and departed.

"Mr. Bentley, you're back?" a man who looked to be a casino worker asked the older gentleman.

"Yes, thank you." He looked to Dakota. "And with my good luck charm." He winked at Dakota. It wasn't a flirty kind of wink. It was more of a smooth one, and this older man was smooth indeed. He wore a nice suit, and shoes that shined so bright, if Dakota got down on all fours and looked at them, she'd probably be able to see her reflection clearly. The watch around his wrist was platinum with diamonds. It all went hand in hand with that mellow scent he'd left behind on the elevator after he had departed.

"Good luck charm, huh?" Dakota said. "And what's that supposed to mean, Mr. Bentley?" She repeated the name she'd heard the casino worker call him.

"You'll see." Mr. Bentley went and stood at the table by the worker. Mr. Bentley took several stacks of the chips that were sitting in front of the worker, who had evidently been keeping an eye on them for their true owner, Mr. Bentley. He then scooted them farther onto the table. Next the dealer gave him the dice and he scooped them up. He nodded for Dakota to come stand next to him.

With raised eyebrows and her lips twisted, she walked over next to Mr. Bentley, her entire demeanor showing how reluctant she was to do so. "Hmmm, let me guess. You want me to blow on your dice or something," Dakota said.

He put his head down and grinned. "Too much of a cliché. Besides, I tried that before with the brunette over there." He nodded toward the table next to them at a medium-height, medium-build lady who was with another woman. "Obviously the whole dice blowing thing only works in movies," he said. "So to answer your question, no, I don't want you to blow my dice for me. I want you to throw my dice for me."

"Me?" Dakota placed her hand against her chest. Too bad she hadn't thought of or had time for a red polish job.

That would have been a nice added touch. Good thing, though, she maintained some pretty decent nails. She at least kept them buffed, so they had a shine to them. "I've never gambled before in my life. With the exception of that slot machine over there." She nodded toward the area where she'd been playing the penny slot. "But you see how that panned out." She sarcastically said, "I won some big money."

"This is different. Those slot machines are rigged for when someone's going to win and when someone is going to lose."

Dakota placed her hands on her hips. "Well I guess you left that out of your little spiel when you were talking me into gambling."

He smiled one of those busted smiles. "I just wanted you to at least give it a try, live a little." He turned to the craps table, smiled, and rubbed it. "But this right here. It's all about luck. And right now I need a little Lady Luck." He took Dakota's hand that still lay subconsciously on her chest. He placed the dice in it. "It's been a long time since I've had a lady's touch."

"I beg to differ. You just had that Kim Kardashian brunette over there touch."

Both Dakota and Mr. Bentley looked at the woman who was fondling all over some gambling older man.

"I'm sure you'll agree with me when I say that that right there, my friend, is no lady."

Dakota laughed and shook her head. "You are so bad."

"Then make me better. Make me a winner," he pleaded. "Like I said, a lady's luck, beginner's luck, just a lady's touch, perhaps that's what I'm missing and need in order to turn my night around." He gazed into her blushing eyes. "So will you do me the honors?" Before Dakota could decline he said, "You wouldn't deny an old man one last pleasure would you?"

"Well since you make it seem like you're on your death-bed, how could I?" Dakota agreed. She turned toward the table. "Now how does this work?"

The gentleman turned and placed both hands on a huge stack of chips. He then pushed them onto the table. "Now you just roll an eleven or seven and I'll be a very rich man."

"And if I don't?" Dakota asked.

"Then I'll be a very poor man and have a lot of explaining to do with my wife."

Dakota looked down and for the first time noticed the man's wedding band. It was his eye-catching watch that had caught her attention earlier.

"Oh, I see," she said. "Well, the last thing I want to do is upset your wife. So if you don't mind, I'd like to blow on the dice anyhow. For one, what harm is a little extra luck? For two, I like clichés. Everyone does, or else they would have never become clichés in the first place."

"And is there a three?" He looked at Dakota knowingly.

She shimmied her shoulders and gave off a huge grin. "Because I've always wanted to do it." On that note, Dakota blew on the dice, looked toward the gentleman, and he gave her a nod letting her know to go for it. She rolled the dice.

The dice seemed to fly in the air and bounce about the table in slow motion as Dakota watched them. Finally they hit the wall of the table and landed flat on the table. Dakota hadn't finished adding up the numbers in her head before she heard the onlookers cheering. The next thing she knew, the dealer was pushing an even bigger heap of chips back at Mr. Bentley, then scooped up the dice. Dakota never even finished counting before the dealer was on to the next bet.

"I guess I did good." Dakota smiled.

"You did better than good." The man took out a cigar and lit it.

"Hey! Stop thief!" Dakota began to yell as she looked over the gentleman's shoulder.

He turned to see a different casino worker gathering all his winnings onto a tray. The casino worker looked to the gentleman, then to the crazy woman doing the name calling, then back to the gentleman. "Mr. Bentley, is everything okay here?"

"Yes. All is fine. Please proceed," he ordered the casino worker, who then placed all of Mr. Bentley's winnings on a tray and disappeared.

"But he's . . . but that's your money."

"Shhh, shhh. It's okay, dear. He's going to credit my account. It's fine."

"Oh." Dakota relaxed. "Well. Thank you for allowing me to play my first game of craps, with your money."

"Yes, but at least you didn't lose my money. Oh, yeah, I almost forgot." Mr. Bentley dug into his pants pocket. "Here you are."

"What is it?" Dakota opened her hand and watched five chips fall into her palm. "Awww. How cute. You don't have to. I assure you I won't be using these. That right there"—she pointed to the craps table—"was luck indeed. Here, you use them since you're the real gambler anyway." She extended them back to Mr. Bentley.

He pushed her hand away. "Oh, no. You keep them. Cash them in. You don't just have to use them to gamble with you know." He leaned in and whispered into her ear. "You can cash them in for face value. It's not play money."

Dakota looked down at the chips, each with $100 on them. Her mouth opened. "But this is . . ." She was at a loss for words.

"Yes, I know." He closed her hand back around the chips. "That's the least I can offer you for what you just won me." He snickered.

Dakota, with a serious expression on her face, replied, "That was just all in fun. I . . . I can't take these and cash them in for money."

"Well, I'm not taking them back. It's gambling etiquette. So if you don't want to cash them in for money, then I suggest you gamble them away."

A frown spread across Dakota's face. "But I'll be all night on the penny slot trying to get rid of these."

Mr. Bentley couldn't help but laugh. "Yes, you would be." He looked around. "I have a suggestion. How about you accompany me for the rest of the evening in there?" He pointed.

Dakota followed his finger to a room with a sign that read HIGH ROLLERS.

"It's where . . ." He paused and thought for a moment. "What you young people might say where the ballers go to have fun in a casino." He winked.

"Oh, I see."

"Yeah, the minimum bets might not be the average gambler's cup of tea. Especially one who's used to the penny slot." The two shared a laugh.

"Well, I don't know." Dakota was hesitant.

"Why not?" Mr. Bentley shrugged.

Dakota looked back over into the room and watched the gamblers. Those people were probably placing single bets that were more than what Dakota had in her savings account. She was anything but a high roller. Why, it wasn't even really her money she'd be betting with. She would be perpetrating a fraud for sure. She truly had to consider whether she was taking this whole stranger within thing too far. Certainly if she pushed her limits, someone would see right through her. She didn't want to look like the oddball who . . . She stopped herself right in her own thoughts. She was wearing a thousand dollar dress for goodness' sake. She would fit in just as much as the next. Dakota and her khakis might not have, but Marie on the other hand was dressed for the occasion. "You are absolutely right; why the hell not?"

"Well then allow me the pleasure." Mr. Bentley did a slight bow and extended his elbow to Dakota.

On second and final thought, Dakota surmised that she wasn't taking the whole Marie thing too far. As a matter of fact, she wasn't taking this Marie thing far enough. And now it was time to see just how far Marie was willing to go. "Why thank you, kind sir. I'd love to." She did a curtsy, looped her arm through the older gentleman's arm, and headed to the high roller's lounge.

Chapter 8

"Five thousand dollars? You're shitting me. That's my baby girl. Ha! You go get 'em, baby."

Dakota had never heard her father so excited for her in his life than hearing that his baby girl had ventured off into the high rollers' territory with $500 in chips and a twenty-eight dollars and thirty cent voucher and came out with $5,000. Beginner's luck for sure. But if she stopped and thought about it long enough, she'd really never brought much excitement his way. He was always whooping and hollering or fussing and cussing over something Billie had done, whether it was something she should have or shouldn't have done. At least she'd garnered his attention. But Dakota couldn't think of one time she had, besides her straight A report card she'd brought home in fifth grade. But then pretty soon, straight As became such a norm for her, it was expected. So there was no longer much excitement. Nope, only a five dollar bill for every A.

"I will, Dad." Dakota smiled as she sat on the chair in her new Rio Masquerade Suite. The hotel had upgraded her. Rolling with the high rollers and accompanying Mr. Bentley had had its perks indeed. Dakota had told the hotel that they could have waited until this morning to do it, but they insisted on the immediate upgrade. So at two o'clock this morning, once she'd ended her night with Mr. Bentley, two bellmen helped her pack up and moved her to her suite. Fortunately for them all, there really wasn't much to pack.

"Can you put Mommy back on the phone?" Dakota asked.

"Sure. I love you."

"Love you too, Pops."

She could hear her father passing the phone to her mother. "Here you go. Dakota wants to speak to you again."

"Thank you," her mother said. "And quit cussin'."

Dakota could just picture her mother swatting her father.

"Hey, Dakota," her mother said once she was on the line.

"Hey, Mom. Well I just wanted to tell you that I love you. Late registration for those who missed last night's and continental breakfast is about to start, so I have to get going."

"All right, dear. You be safe. I love you."

"Love you too, Mom." Dakota ended the call. She looked down at her phone at the time. It was almost eight o'clock. Today's registration was about to begin. A continental breakfast was being offered as well. Opening remarks were at nine and the first official session would begin at nine-thirty.

Dakota sat in the chair in the living area wrapped in the hotel robe. She was trying to figure out exactly what to do. While shopping at the Forum Shops the day before, she had not only forgotten to purchase undergarments, but she'd forgotten to purchase something to wear for today's sessions as well.

"That damn Billie," she cussed out loud. She leaned her head back against the chair and exhaled.

She'd already registered so she didn't have to worry about being there for that. She'd grabbed a sandwich before retiring to bed so she wasn't really hungry with that still weighing on her. Continental breakfast definitely wasn't an issue. Opening remarks of conferences usually consisted of someone bragging about how one person or another single-handedly or with the help of many put the conference together. There were many acknowledgments and thanks. She could read the program for all that. So in that instant she hopped up, went to the bathroom, showered, and put on her khakis and the underwear she'd at least had the decency to rinse out in the sink and hang over the shower bar to dry in the middle of the night. She then put on her bra and the shirt she had traveled to Las Vegas in. She pulled her hair back in a "just to get it off my neck" 'do, threw on her shoes, grabbed her purse, and was out the door. Hopefully Lady Luck was still with her and she could find at least a gift shop or something that was open this early in the morning.

She got on the elevator and went back to the floor where she'd purchased the lip gloss and earrings. That particular store was closed, but there was a twenty-four-hour gift shop open. And that was it. With no other options really, Dakota went to the gift shop. Thank God Las Vegas was not only Sin City and a gamble town, but a lot of conferences were held there and a lot of golfing, which meant golf shirts.

"Guess today I'm going to have to be one of the guys," Dakota said as she began to pick through the limited collection of golf polos. All the cutesy pink ones only went up to an extra large. Dakota probably could have gotten into the adult extra large, but she liked her clothes to fit loosely. So, just as Aquilla had pointed out on the shopping rendezvous, she always bought her clothes slightly big.

Dakota put down the extra-large pink polo that had the name of the hotel and logo on the upper left hand side instead of a jockey riding a horse. She found herself having to go through the men's polos that went all the way up to a size 3X. She found a white one in a double X. She held it up and figured this was the closest she was going to get to still at least feeling like a woman even though she would be wearing a man's shirt. Just as she was about to walk away from the clothing rack she stopped. She turned and looked back over her shoulder at the pink extra-large polo. She eyeballed the white men's double X, then cast her eyes back to the pink one.

With a mischievous grin, she quickly went and placed the white polo back on the rack and grabbed the pink one. She held it up, and before taking it over to the counter to pay for it said, "Yep, Marie, I think you're going to look good in this."

Twenty minutes after purchasing the pink shirt, Dakota was exiting the elevator on the floor of where the first session was to be held. She'd gone back to her suite to change into her shirt and then went straight back down to the conference. Her khakis would have to hold up for one more day.

She could hear applause coming from the main ballroom and then she heard voices begin to chat. Opening remarks had just ended; her timing was perfect. Noticing the continental breakfast area was still set up, Dakota walked over there and began fixing herself a cup of coffee. Attendees began to file out of the ballroom and into the main lobby area. Several met her over at the serving area and began fixing themselves a morning kick or grabbing some of the remaining pastries. The sheese cream Danish did look tasty. After putting her condiments into her coffee, Dakota decided to grab one filled with lemon.

"I see you plan on skipping out early for a game of golf," a gentleman whispered as he poured himself a cup of coffee.

"Pardon me?" Dakota had no idea where that had come from; left field, perhaps.

"Your shirt. You golf?"

Dakota looked down at her pink golf shirt with the hotel logo on it. "Oh, this. Well . . . it's a long story." One that she did not feel like explaining.

"Darn." He snapped his finger. "I was just certain I'd found someone who could teach me a thing or two on the green."

Dakota's eyes screamed confusion.

"The golf course. The green," he said. "You don't golf at all, huh?"

"Guilty," Dakota confessed. "I'm afraid not. Never golfed in my life."

"Oh, you should try it then."

"It looks like such a serious sport. I don't know anyone who would have the patience to teach me."

The man held his arms out wide. "You're looking at him."

"But didn't you just say you were looking for someone to teach you? Oh how quickly we go from being the student to the teacher."

"Hey, anytime I get to be on the green with someone who's going to make my game look good, I'm all for it." He and Dakota laughed. "But seriously. I honestly wouldn't mind. Golf is fun. No, it's not all physical like basketball or football, but it's fun. Challenges you more mentally than physically."

"Well, that's a plus for me, because I really don't like to get that physical," Dakota said.

"Oh, I see." The man's cheeks flushed red and the blond hairs on his arms, sticking out from his own golf shirt, stood up.

Dakota tried to pretend as though she hadn't noticed. She felt bad for making him uncomfortable. She did a quick save. "Well, I guess it wouldn't hurt to learn something new. I hear a lot of business deals are made on the golf court anyway."

"It's course."

"Excuse me?"

"It's golf course. You said court."

"Oh. Yikes." Dakota put her hand over her mouth, which didn't don the red lip gloss this morning. "Sure you can work with a beginner like me?"

"Ahhhh, I think I can handle it. What do you say we give it a shot this afternoon? The last session ends at four and then I think there is networking and a recap. What do you say we skip the networking and hit the course? I'll schedule us a tee time."

"Do you mean play hooky on the very first day of class?" Dakota whispered playfully.

"I'm a bad influence. What can I say?" He laughed.

"Sure. I guess I'm dressed for it. I'll just run my bag back up to my room and meet you, what, out where you catch a taxi?"

"That's fine, but I have a rental, so I'll just pick you up around there and we'll head to the course. But let's make it three forty-five. "

Dakota thought for a minute. "Wait, but the last session doesn't even end until four."

"Yeah, but William Staudimeier is speaking at that session. He's not long-winded. He always finishes up early."

"Well, okay." Dakota sounded slightly hesitant. She didn't want to end up having to be rude and walk out in the middle of a presentation just so she wouldn't keep her golf partner waiting. But reluctantly, she agreed. "Sounds like a plan then. I'll meet you downstairs at three forty-five. Oh, and I didn't even get your name."

"Sorry about that." He set his tote down on the ground then shook hands with Dakota with his hand that was coffee free. "I'm William—"

Before he could say another word, Dakota looked down at his badge. "William Staudimeier. Real funny, Mr. Staudimeier." She rolled her eyes upward and smiled.

He smiled back. "That's me. Sorry, didn't mean to mess with you like that."

"Oh, it's okay. I don't mind a sense of humor."

"Great." He clasped his hands together and rocked back and forth. "Well, anyway, I'm going to go say hello to a couple colleagues I see. Enjoy the day's sessions."

"Same to you," Dakota replied, while noticing him looking down at her chest. Dakota slightly turned away and subconsciously covered her breast. She did have on a bra today, so she was certain her nipples weren't poking out drawing any attention. So this man was some kind of bold to be outright looking at her boobies, she thought.

Realizing how tense and uncomfortable Dakota appeared to be all of a sudden, William took note and put his hands up. "Oh, no, pardon me, forgive me." He put his hands up and shook them. "I was, uh, looking for your name badge. I didn't get your name either."

"Ohhhh." Dakota, smiled, exhaled, and then relaxed. She looked down at her own chest in search of her nametag, realizing it was still in her tote. "Marie. You can call me Marie."

"Fine. Take care, Marie. Downstairs. Three forty-five." He tapped his watch. "Don't be late."

"Three forty-five on the dot," Dakota reiterated and watched him walk away. She exhaled when he was no longer in her presence. She wanted to die. She'd made a date with a complete stranger. A date to get in a car and drive off with a complete stranger. Fuck Marie. That bitch wasn't about to have her found cut up with her head severed to be found in the desert. There was living a carefree life and then there was being stupid . . . and dying!

As Dakota made her way to the room in which the conference's first session would take place, her belly ached with nervousness. She no longer had an appetite for the Danish, so she set it on the table in the back of the room that had pitchers of ice water and glasses for the attendees to help themselves. Still somewhat in a daze at the date she'd just made with a stranger, she went and flopped down at one of the tables that wasn't yet occupied. How the hell was she going to get out of her golf date?

Within minutes all the tables began to fill. There were smiles and nods among those at Dakota's table. A couple of the people chatted as if they knew one another. Dakota would have made an attempt to engage herself in a conversation, but she was too preoccupied with how to go about standing up Mr. Staudimeier.

Eventually the speaker of the hour was introduced and got right into his topic of discussion. Dakota half listened, taking random notes. In between her business-related notes were notes of ideas of how to get out of her date with death. She'd write a suggestion down, then moments later scratch it off her list for one reason or another.

That's it! she thought. *He's no stranger. I'm the stranger.* She had to remind herself that her Vegas trip wasn't about complete logic. Sure she had to use wisdom, and she would. But everything in life didn't have to have logic attached to it. Why did there always have to be a reason to just do something carefree? *It's the 'just because,' or the 'because I can' that makes life exciting.*

Chances were, any guy she went out on a first date with would pretty much be a stranger. Even after talking to someone for hours on the phone, you still can't tell if they are a rapist, mass murderer, or something. You gotta go out there and get to know people and discern the type of

person they are. When it came to William, Dakota didn't
have that kind of time nor did she need it. She'd spent
all of five minutes with him and anticipated spending
about another hour with him during his session. That
would have to be enough. Did she really need to invest
more time than that anyway into someone she'd never
see again after returning home? So with that reasoning,
she decided she would not break her date with William.
That would also eliminate her having to avoid him for the
remainder of the conference after having stood him up.

She was going to go golfing for the first time in her
life and she was going to have fun. With that settled,
Dakota was able to pay attention to the speaker, take
some real notes, and even participate in a little Q&A. As
her stomach growled she couldn't help but think, *damn;
where is that Danish?*

Chapter 9

After making a fifteen-minute pit stop to her room before heading downstairs to meet William, Dakota was walking through the casino fully energized. Her sleep last night had been just what she needed to get her body on track and on beat with the three-hour time zone difference. The sessions had been very enlightening. She'd actually learned quite a bit that she could take back to work, share with her team, and help them better the service on the job. William, specifically, had been very inspiring. He gave good tips and was one heck of a motivational speaker. Dakota could only hope he could motivate her to get a strike, first and ten, hole in one, or whatever the right golf terminology was.

She walked outside the transportation area and looked around. William had told her he'd be in a silver full-size car. He couldn't remember the exact make and model of the rental. Dakota looked but didn't see any silver cars. She didn't have his cell phone number to call him. Or, maybe she did.

At the end of William's session, he'd made his business card available to the attendees. Dakota had made sure to grab one. This was where wisdom came in. During her pit stop back at her suite she'd quickly called her sister to let her know a little of what was going on.

"I'm going for a game of golf," Dakota had told her sister.

"But, girl, you never go golfing," Billie had said. "Do you even know the slightest thing about golf besides the fact that Tiger Woods plays?"

"Who?" Dakota asked.

Billie was just about to answer her until she realized her sister was being sarcastic. "Forget you."

Dakota sighed.

"Sorry. It's just that I've never known you to have the slightest interests in . . . Oh, I get it. Doing something new. You're taking my advice. See, told you. Isn't it exciting?"

"Yeah, yeah, whatever." Dakota brushed her sister's excitement off and got to her point. "Take this name down."

"Wait. Hold on. Let me get a pen and paper." There was some shuffling around while Billie retrieved a writing utensil and something to write on. "Okay, go."

Dakota proceeded to read off William's information from his business card. "So that's who I'll be with. If you don't hear from me by the end of the night, call 911."

"Girl, stop being so dramatic. You're letting Daddy and all that ID Channel business get you all worked up."

"You darn right. I'm all the way here in Las Vegas by myself. I'm putting myself in the perfect scenario to be the starring subject for one of those episodes. But anyway, I'm also going to leave a note on the hotel stationary as well. At least housekeeping will know who raped and mutilated me." Dakota sighed.

"Oh, stop it and go golfing for crying out loud. It will be fun."

"Yeah, but that's because you like to golf." Dakota knew her sister attended the charity golf outings her boyfriend's fraternity put on quite a bit.

"No, it's because I like the beer cart." Billie laughed. "The beer cart is the best part."

"Figures. Anyway, I gotta go, sis. Give Mom and Dad my love the next time you talk with them."

"I will. Love you and be safe."

Now as Dakota stood there waiting for William, she wondered if the phone number on his business card that she had given Billie was his office or cell phone number. Most people included both on their business cards nowadays. She pulled the card out of her purse but was startled by the light beep of a horn. She looked up to see a Chrysler 300 and William waving.

William put the car in park and then got out to open the passenger door for Dakota. "Marie. You didn't stand me up."

"Of course not." Dakota smiled as William patted her on the back. "Why would I?"

"Well, I wasn't sure if I'd bored you so badly during my presentation that you'd want to get and stay as far away from this snoozer as you could." He feigned a yawn and put his hand over his mouth.

"Please, you were great." She shooed her hand.

"Well thank you." He took a modest bow.

Dakota slid inside the open door, lifting her left leg and then her right. William looked a little concerned as he stood there holding the door.

"What?" Dakota asked.

"Do you really plan on doing any golfing, or just hanging out at the bar in the lounge?" He looked down at her feet. "Or are you going to golf in those shoes? I mean, they're pretty nice shoes, but for golfing . . ."

Dakota looked down at the black two-inch-heel loafer-type shoes she'd worn to Vegas. The only other shoes she had were the pumps she'd purchased at the store at Caesars Palace. Those wouldn't suffice either.

"Darn it the snabbits." Dakota sucked her teeth. "I forgot I don't have any shoes to golf in." She looked up at William with disappointed eyes, fixing to get out of the car.

"Well, I'm sure they have some kind of gift shop, store, or something on the grounds. You should be able to find something there."

"You think?" Dakota squinted her face doubtfully. By this time she'd placed both feet back outside of the car, planning to nix the whole golf idea completely.

"I'm sure they'll have something for you. If not, the grass may feel good underneath your feet and between your toes."

Just the thought of something as corny as that brought out just a little bit of the old Dakota within. Now running barefoot through the grass, that was fun and exciting to wallflower Dakota. Marie had to quit being selfish and let Dakota have a little fun. So Dakota swung her feet back inside the vehicle, got nice and situated in the passenger seat, and waited for William to close her door. William then walked back around to the driver's side, climbed in, and after the two buckled up, followed the instructions of the GPS to the golf course where they'd be spending the rest of the afternoon.

"Yippee!" Dakota jumped up and down after getting the ball into the ninth hole.

"Not bad," William complimented. "You're a natural."

"No, you're just a good teacher," Dakota said to him.

"Correction, you are a good student. And I give you an A for effort and participation. Now what do you say we go back inside to the restaurant and celebrate your grade card over dinner, on me?"

Because Dakota was a beginner, he'd only signed them up for nine holes, but with how well she'd done, they could have easily gone the full eighteen. Well, maybe not the full eighteen, but close enough to it.

"Dinner on the teacher? Oh, how sweet." Dakota rubbed her stomach. "I am a little hungry."

"Good, then let's go hang up our cleats." William began to gather all the clubs and balls while Dakota just stood there with a puzzled look on her face. "Ahhh, gotcha. Just wanted to see if you were paying attention."

Dakota started laughing. "Good, because I was thinking . . ." She put her index finger to her temple in thought. "Don't football players wear cleats too?"

"You've just earned yourself some bonus points. Guess dessert is on me as well."

After gathering all their things, they hopped in the golf cart and headed back to the lobby. Once inside, they each went to their respective restroom to wash their hands, then met at the restaurant.

Once seated, their drink orders were taken, then they conversed while browsing the menu.

"The grilled tilapia sounds good. I think I'm going to try that," Dakota said.

"I've never really liked fish. I think I'm going to try the jambalaya with polish sausage." He moved the menu from covering his face and said to Dakota with a serious mug, "Now I like polish sausage." He winked then scanned the menu one last time just to be sure. "Yep, that's exactly what I'm going to have." He closed the menu and put it down just as the waiter brought their drinks to them.

"Do you need a little more time, or do you know what you want?" the waiter asked.

"I think we are ready." William looked to Dakota for confirmation.

"Oh, yes. We're ready," Dakota said to the waiter.

The couple placed their orders, handed the waiter their menus and then went back to talking. "So, Marie. Where are you from?" William asked after taking a sip of his seltzer water.

"Michigan." Dakota took a sip of her limeade.

"Detroit."

"No. Flint."

"Born and raised?"

"Yes, sir."

"Oh, don't call me, sir. You make me feel like my father."

They laughed and made a little more small talk until the waiter brought out their food. They ate, laughed, and joked over their meal. Dakota hadn't laughed that hard since Kevin Hart's *Let Me Explain*.

"You have a wonderful sense of humor," Dakota said, wiping tears from her eyes from laughing so hard. "I really like that about you." She swallowed then wiped her mouth with her napkin. "Can I tell you something?"

"Sure," William said, wiping his mouth as he chewed his food.

"I thought you were going to be a stiff."

"I can't blame you. The speaker at an insurance conference. Whooo hoo. What a ball of fun," he joked about himself.

"Oh, stop it. I didn't mean all that. But you are a pleasant surprise. Like I said, your sense of humor is amazing. So entertaining. I can't imagine a dull moment with you."

"Ahhh." He raised his fork. "My partner says that same thing about me."

"Partner? You own your own business aside from the work you do for your company?"

"Well, the company I do work for is my company. But I don't have any business partners. I meant my life partner, Rodney."

Dakota stopped her fork midair. "Oh."

William tried to read her facial expression but couldn't. "Is there a problem?"

"No, it's just that . . ." Dakota carefully organized her words. "It's just that I had no idea."

He snapped his finger. "Oh, shoot, I did forget to have them put it on my name badge. William Staudimeier: Gay . . . and not the happy gay."

Dakota laughed. "Well I agree with Rodney. You are a riot." Dakota finished up her meal then pushed her plate away.

William had already finished. "So you're not one of those chicks with a so-called gaydar, huh?" Rodney used his fingers to make quotation marks.

"Obviously not. Here I thought I was going to have to fight you off of me on the golf course. Come to find I'm not even your cup of tea." Dakota snapped her finger and feigned disappointment.

"Yeah, right. Like you would have been interested in a middle-aged white man."

"Can I share something with you?" Dakota leaned in and said almost in a whisper.

"Sure."

"Last night I was just a teensy weensy bit interested in an old man from India."

"No way." William looked surprised. "An old man. Girl, do you have any idea how disgusted you would be after a night of sex with him, only to wake up to his saggy booty?"

Dakota burst out laughing. She put her napkin in front of her mouth in just enough time to spit her limeade in it. "You are crazy."

"No, you are crazy if you want me to believe you were going to get busy with an old Indian man."

"A man from India," Dakota corrected him.

"Whatever, still I say no way."

"Yes way. I don't know if it was the fact that he had all this money, even gave me five hundred dollars in gambling chips, but I was feeling the old man."

"Whoa, big spender. Now I get it. Hell, think I've got a chance with this fella?"

"Nah. He was married."

"And? That never stopped about half of the men I've dated."

Dakota shook her head. "You know, I have nothing against gay men or women. Seriously. But the whole down low thing bothers me so much. Why not just be who you are and be proud of it?"

"Umm, I wouldn't say it's that easy." William put his hand up to stop the press. "Not that I'm saying I agree with the down low thing, because I don't. But being gay isn't, like I alluded to earlier, something you just put on a nametag and wear proudly. There is such a stigma attached. Society is something else." He shook his head as if reflecting on instances he wished he could forget.

"Tell me about it," Dakota agreed. "People ask me all the time, 'What are you?' I know they do that about my race, but what if it gets to the point where people start asking that about someone's sexuality?"

"You know what? I wouldn't be mad if they did. If it becomes that common, then maybe all the hate would dissipate to some degree."

Dakota thought for a moment and then nodded. "Yeah, you have a point, William."

"Can I get you guys dessert or anything?" their waiter walked over to the table and asked.

"Uhhh." Dakota looked to William.

"That double fudge sundae looked pretty good."

"I know. I saw that." Dakota licked her lips and rubbed her belly. "But it looked like so much. I'd waste mine."

"Yeah, me too." William looked to be changing his mind about getting it. Then he thought for a moment. "Hey, why don't we split one?" His eyes lit up again. "You come sit over here by me." He slid over and patted the empty space next to him. "And we'll share it. What do you say?"

"I say I hope Rodney doesn't mind me double dipping with his man."

The two laughed as Dakota got up.

"I'll put the order in right away." The waiter smiled and then walked off.

Dakota sat next to William and the two continued speaking on the whole race and sexuality issue until their sundae arrived.

"This looks delicious," Dakota said as she took the first scoop. Hot fudge dripped from her spoon.

"It does." William took a scoop. "Rodney would be fit to be tied if he knew he wasn't my first."

Dakota almost choked on a nut that had been sprinkled on the sundae. "Excuse me. Where did that come from?"

William covered his mouth. "Oh, no, I didn't mean that. I just mean that I've never even shared a dessert with him before. This is so nice."

"Well, I'm glad we could create this milestone together, William. I'm honored."

Next they each took a scoop at the same time. They looked at each other, thinking the same thing William said, "To a first."

"To a first," Dakota concurred as they finished off their dessert.

Chapter 10

Day two in Vegas had been just as eventful as day one. Worn out from a day of seminars followed by an hour and a half on the golf course, and then dinner with William, truly Dakota felt she had every right to climb in her bed and tap out for the night, even if it was only eight o'clock. If she didn't do anything else, Dakota still had to hit the store and buy her some underwear.

She was definitely going to Ross this time. She'd had to buy a pair of Keds to golf in from the store on site at the golf course. She paid almost fifty dollars for a pair of shoes she probably could have gotten for half the price at a regular store. That definitely cut into her shopping money. Even with her big win last night, she still wanted to at least try to stay somewhere within the vicinity of her budget. Now if she did end up going over, she'd blame that on Marie too, along with anything else she might regret while in Sin City.

So after catching her breath for a few minutes, she went to the elevator to hail a taxi to Ross. And forty minutes later, she was paying her fare and heading into Ross. She couldn't believe all the traffic along the strip. What she thought should have been only a ten- or fifteen-minute ride seemed like forever. She had almost gotten out of that taxi and put those Keds to more use. But, instead, she just stayed in the taxi and people-watched.

It only took her an hour to find a nice outfit for tomorrow and the day after that. She'd hit the mall for some play clothes for whenever she got a chance to experience Vegas nightlife. She got some undergarments, fancy name-brand ones for a discounted price, and a cute shirt-like gown. She found a nice pair of shoes and some great value jewelry pieces. She decided she'd hit a specialty store in the mall for any smell goods and bath products, although in the bathroom of her suite awaited a nice full-size spa collection, unlike the sample sizes that had been in her original room. That spa set might actually suffice. The products were so amazing, she could almost taste them. She even felt yummy after cleansing with them. She just hadn't gone completely through the entire spa basket yet, so no telling what other delicious feel good products awaited her.

While standing in the check-out line she spotted this silky black clutch with black stones beaded across the front. It must have been waiting there just for her. Her play clothes would definitely have to coordinate with that. She quickly scooped the little clutch up into her arms along with her other items. She was one of those women you still saw walking around the store every now and then with an armful of clothes versus pushing a buggy around. That was too much like exercise for Dakota. Plus she hated trying to maneuver those carts through stores such as Ross with those small aisles and tons of people trying to luck up on a deal, especially here in Vegas. To her, that was equivalent to mothers trying to fight a crowd at outdoor festivals with a baby stroller. Why bother?

Dakota was back at the hotel by 9:30 p.m. She'd made a mental note to attend the Carnival Buffett, which she'd be able to enjoy for free thanks to Mr. Bentley having had his little casino helper sign her up for a player's card. But tonight it would be room service. Heck, she was $5,000 richer than when she'd come to Vegas. *Hell, I could have bought a different-color pair of Keds for every day of the week,* she said after thinking about her financial windfall. *I can still be a bit freer with my ducats without being frugal and fruitless.* She was going to make up for her most recent backsliding when it came to being a tight wad on room service. She wasn't even going to look at the price, just the food and what she had a taste for.

She entered her hotel suite, dropped her bags, and dashed to the bathroom to get a nice shower and put on some pajamas and clean underwear. Thank goodness she wouldn't have to sleep naked like she'd had to last night.

Dakota stuffed herself into the size extra-large pajamas that fit snug around every inch. She couldn't help but stare at herself in the mirror for a moment. She'd never really noticed just how curvy she was. Yes, she was thick, but in all the right places. She should have been telling people her name was Juicy, because that's how she felt. For years she'd been hiding all this up under big clothes, when if she'd just worn her true size, she could have been showing off every nook, cranny, and curve and, at the same time, have done her full figure some justice.

The lone tear streaming down Dakota's face caught her off-guard. Where were all these emotions coming from? She felt like she should have been a cast member in the movie *The Best Man Holiday.* Every damn body in that movie cried a river. But she couldn't help it. Although her sister had no idea the depths of it when she said it, Dakota truly was a stranger to herself. Why didn't she know what her body looked like? If she'd been so okay with who she was and all her thickness, why had she avoided stopping in front of the mirror and taking note of it, showing her own self some deserving attention? Never mind about the woulda, shoulda, coulda. Today was a new day.

"No more," Dakota whispered to herself before wiping the tear away, turning off the bathroom light and going to order her room service.

Thirty minutes later, Dakota's gourmet popcorn and cherry Coke, her midnight snack, was delivered. It was billed to her room, but she tipped the delivery guy five dollars.

She found one of her favorite reality shows and indulged. Five minutes after finishing her snack she was knocked out across the bed, dreaming of what awaited her on day three.

Dakota couldn't have been more grateful she'd requested a wakeup call before closing her eyes for the final time last night. At first she decided against it figuring she was going to bed early enough that her body would wake up on its own. That second thought was the reason why she would be on time to her eight o'clock session. The ringing phone had awoken her from a dead sleep. No way would she have gotten up on her own.

After brushing her teeth, washing her face, and doing her hair, Dakota was all set. She grabbed her tote and headed down to her session. She passed on the continental breakfast, hell-bent on experiencing that buffet later today. She was going to eat up some stuff, so she wanted to save all her calories for the buffet. So instead of one of those tasty Danishes with cream cheese icing drizzled about and a fruit filling, she fixed herself a cup of coffee that gave her just enough boost to stay fully awake for the next two hour-and-a-half sessions, with a break in between.

At last, it was lunchtime. Lunch break was an hour and a half. Dakota figured that would be plenty of time to enjoy the buffet, but was disappointed when she was told it didn't open until four o'clock in the afternoon. Once again she could have had a frickin' Danish. She made a mental note that tomorrow she was going to get a Danish whether she was hungry for it or not. Even if it had to set in her purse and she devoured it on her flight back home, she was going to enjoy her a Danish.

Dakota decided to just grab her a chef salad and call to check in with her family and friends while she sat in the little café and ate.

"Don't forget to bring me back a shot glass," Trice reminded Dakota as the two talked on the phone. "You know I collect those. Every time somebody on my team goes on vacation I always have them bring me back a shot glass."

"I know," Dakota said, picking an egg yolk out of her salad and placing it in her mouth. "I haven't even gone souvenir shopping yet, but I'll be sure to get it."

"Well your flight leaves tomorrow afternoon doesn't it?"

"Yes. The last session ends at eleven in the morning. My flight leaves out at three or four. I have to double check my itinerary."

"Dang, you won't even get back to Michigan until late tomorrow night."

"I know; then I have to turn around and go in to work the next day. Blah."

"I'm sure you'll be all right. God knows you are down there getting plenty of rest." Trice laughed.

Dakota didn't even get mad at yet another reference to her being a wallflower. She just shook her head and thought, *if only you knew, girlfriend. If only you knew.* "Well, let me get off this phone. I have to get back to my next session in a few and I want to check in with my mom and dad before I do."

"Okay, girlie. If I don't talk to you before you get back, enjoy your last night in Vegas and do everything I would do," Trice expressed.

Chuckling Dakota replied, "Okay, Trice. Love ya."

"Love you too."

They ended the call. Dakota ate more of her salad before calling her parents. There wasn't an answer on the house phone, so she ended up having to reach her mother on her cell. She checked in, finished up that phone call, and then finished up her salad. She headed back to her afternoon sessions where she was totally engaged. She interacted with a couple of people she'd spoken to and had networked with over the course of the last couple of days.

Too bad William wasn't there. She missed his company already. William had only been there as a hired speaker and not someone who was attending the full conference. So when they returned to the hotel, they said their good-byes at the elevator and parted ways. Dakota had actually even gotten teary-eyed. But now it was time to move on to whatever may come.

When five o'clock rolled around, Dakota was grateful. That last speaker had been a complete drag. Dakota almost never drank coffee after the noon hour, but she'd put away two in the last hour and a half trying to stay awake. Not because she was tired, but because the speaker had bored her so.

When she arrived back up to her suite she brushed her teeth. That stale and bitter aftertaste from afternoon coffee was the worst; not to mention it had turned her breath into a deadly weapon that was assaulting everybody she opened her mouth to speak to. But at least it had energized her. She was all set to hit the mall. She wanted to grab something to wear this evening because she planned on trying to catch a show. She also wanted to get her souvenir shopping out of the way. Tomorrow's schedule was going to be too tight to try to squeeze it in then. And she didn't want to get gypped by paying airport souvenir prices. That wasn't being her old frugal self. That was just, once again, using her wisdom.

She just had one day to go in Vegas. Hopefully wisdom would keep her out of any crazy predicaments for the duration of her stay. Only time would tell.

Chapter 11

Dakota was able to pick up a nice maxi dress at Macy's. In passing the makeup counter, one of the clerks even convinced her of getting a free facial and makeover. Dakota had never had one of those before. She felt like a reality television star who had made it big and now people were paying her top dollar to make club appearances. A glam squad had been assigned to get her all dolled up for the night. Her only concern was making sure that when she took a shower back at her suite that she didn't get her face wet. Perhaps she'd have to bathe. On second thought, she couldn't imagine that either Dakota or Marie would ever bathe in a hotel tub. She quivered at the thought.

On her way back in from the mall, she stopped at the concierge desk and asked his assistance in finding a show to attend.

"Oooh, a dinner and a sword fight. That sounds great," Dakota said. She then frowned. "But shoot. I still have my comp for the Carnival Buffet I haven't gotten to use." Dakota was a big girl, but not big enough to have room for two dinners, especially when one was a buffet.

"Perhaps you can go over to the player's club service desk and get them to swap out something; perhaps switch it for a show ticket instead. You never know."

"You're right. What do I have to lose?"

Dakota followed the concierge's advice. And he was right; they gladly worked it out where she could go see the show of her preference.

"Here you are, Ms. Smith; two tickets," the lady at the desk said. "Enjoy the show."

"Thank you, I will." Dakota took the tickets and went up to her suite. Once there she laid out all her new purchases. She was all set for the night. The show seemed like it might be exciting and her intention was to always go to the show by herself. But that was until she was given two tickets. A smile appeared on her lips at just the thought of her and William enjoying the show together. He would have been great company and appreciated it.

While it was on her mind, Dakota decided she'd swap out her purses right now. She went and got the black clutch she'd purchased at Ross and sat down on her bed. She took things out of the tote and her purse and placed what she'd need in the clutch.

Next, she decided to maybe make some calls. Instead of trolling her call log, she went straight to contacts. The only phone number she knew by heart was her parents'. Everyone else changed their phone numbers every other week it seemed. So she stopped wasting memory cells and just used her call log or favorites. In scrolling down her contact list something hit her like a lightning bolt.

"Leon," she said as she came across his name. And just like that, a light bulb went off in her head. She bit her bottom lip as she flicked herself upside the head. Should she or shouldn't she call him and invite him to the show? There really were no pros or cons for either. She hadn't paid a dime for the tickets so there really wouldn't be a financial loss. It's just that she hated that someone else could be enjoying the show. So with nothing to lose, she pressed the little green phone icon and waited for it to start ringing. It ended up going to voicemail. The 1-800 number she'd dialed was clearly a work extension of some sort.

Now here Dakota was once again at another dilemma. Should she leave a message? By the time she'd decided against it, it was too late. The beep signaling for her to leave a message had already chimed.

"Well, uh, you aren't a man of many words I see," she joked in reference to the fact that all his greeting said was, "This is Leon. Leave a message." The beep then immediately followed.

"Well, Leon. This is M—"

Before she could say another word, her other line was beeping in. She looked down at the caller ID screen and saw that it was Leon calling her back. She clicked over. "I was just leaving you a message."

"I'm sorry. Someone at this number just called my phone."

"Oh," Dakota said, realizing that she hadn't even identified herself. It wasn't like her number was locked in his phone. "This is Marie. You met me at—"

"Oh, Marie, I need not be reminded," Leon said. "I'd never forget when and where I was the first time I met Marie."

"You are too funny." She laughed. "Well, I was calling to see . . ." She paused for a moment. "First off, are you still in Vegas?"

"Yes. My flight doesn't head out until tomorrow."

"Well, if you're not busy tonight, I just happen to have an extra ticket to a show. I think it's at the Luxor Hotel . . . the Excalibur, or something like that."

"What time?

"Nine o'clock. Oh, wait. I think dinner is at eight and the show starts at nine. Or maybe you eat during the show." She scrambled for the tickets and then looked them over. "Well, whatever it is, it starts at eight-thirty." She looked over at the digital clock on the nightstand. "Hmmm. I guess that gives us less than an hour. Not much of a notice, so I'll understand if you can't make it."

"Actually, I was about to head down to the sports bar at the hotel I'm staying at and grab a bite there, watch the game, throw back a couple of brews."

"Oh, well, I definitely don't want to intrude on your manly moment."

They both laughed.

"Awww, you got jokes I see."

"A little bit."

"You must keep your friends back home well entertained."

"Wellllll . . ." *If he only knew.*

"But, umm, sure. Who goes to Vegas without catching a show? I'd love to join you."

"Great. Since time is of the essence, how about we just meet there? Is that okay with you?"

"Sure."

"I usually like to be a little early, but I'm probably not going to make it there until around eight forty-five exactly."

"That works for me."

"Fine, then I'll see you then."

"Wait, which hotel is it at?"

"Oh, yeah, that's right." She looked at the tickets again. "Excalibur."

"Fine, I'll meet you there."

Dakota ended the call and then darted to the shower. She made sure to keep the double head massage showerhead on low pressure so that it wouldn't splash on her face and ruin her makeover.

Fifty-five minutes later Dakota was dressed, had coordinated her jewelry, hailed a taxi, and was approaching the theatre doors for the *Tournament of Kings* dinner show.

"And with no time to spare," she heard a voice say.

She looked up and spotted Leon looking all dapper in a nice sweater that was just thick enough to fight off that Vegas evening breeze. He had on some midnight blue crisp creased jeans and was carrying a satchel. Dakota always loved a man bold enough to carry what she referred to as a man purse.

"Well hello, Mr. Rico Suave." She gave him an obvious once-over and then circled him like she was the lioness and he was the prey.

"I knew I was meeting you here"—he pretended to be popping his collar—"so I knew I needed to bring my A game."

Dakota play patted/punched him on the shoulder and went in for a hug. When she felt his arms around her and lightly squeeze her back, she was almost shocked at the fact that she'd even instigated the hug. A hint of doubt and embarrassment crept in and caused her to pull away. She didn't want him to think she was desperate. Or a ho. Or a desperate ho. "So, uh, shall we head in?"

"Yes, we shall." Leon guided Dakota with his hand on her back. They turned in their tickets and were seated.

"This is sooooo cool," Dakota said as she looked around, feeling as though she'd been transported into medieval times. "It's so lifelike."

"Well, it is real. I hear they are supposed to have like real horses and everything."

Dakota's eyes lit up as she continued to admire the place. Shortly thereafter they were given their options of a three-course meal. They ordered and their drinks were brought to them.

"This place is really filled up," Leon said.

"Yes. The man at the hotel said it was popular. We were a little late, but I'm just glad we didn't miss anything."

They drank their beverages. Leon had ordered that brewski he would have had at the sport's bar. They chatted a bit while they waited on their meals to be brought out.

"So, Leon," Dakota started, "where are you from?"

"Your entrees," the waiter said as she placed their meals in front of them.

They oohed and ahhed over the meal that they ate with their fingers for authenticity of the time period. Before long the show started and they watched in amazement as maidens danced, armies fought, including some jousting. There were even fireworks.

Dakota felt like she was right in the middle of a fairytale, not just because she was at this show. Her entire trip to Vegas had been like a fairytale, something a real person in the real world could have only dreamt. And she never wanted to wake up. But just like Cinderella, instead of the clock striking twelve midnight, it would be striking twelve noon and she'd be packing up to head back home. The fairytale would be over. But for now, she was still living it . . . and she was going to live it to the fullest indeed.

Chapter 12

"That was so amazing!" Dakota said as they exited the show.

"That was pretty nice if I do say so myself."

Dakota play tickled him. "Oh just admit it was awesome. I won't strip you of your man card. I know it wasn't a beer with the fellas at the sports bar, but it was nice."

"I said it was nice."

"You said pretty nice. It's not the same. You're trying to downplay it and hide how much you really enjoyed getting taken in by la-la land."

"Yeah, those strobe lights were pretty cool," he admitted. "All right, so it was cool." He put his head down and smiled.

"See, I knew it. Don't worry, Leon, you can keep it real around me."

"Oh can I now?" he looked up at Dakota and said.

"Sure you can," she said as they talked and walked.

He stopped in his tracks and turned to face her. Dakota, sensing he had stopped, followed suit.

"I don't want you to go. I want to spend the night with you."

"What?" Dakota sounded shocked, appalled, surprised, flattered, and everything in between. Hell, she didn't know exactly how she felt. But she did feel some kind of way.

"Oh, no, not like that. I don't want to get with you." He scrunched his face up.

Dakota's jaw dropped. Now she knew exactly how she felt: hurt, sad, insulted, pissed! Had this man just told her to her face she was an ugly, fat cow who he wouldn't fuck with somebody else's dick? Never mind what he said; that's what she heard. She took a deep breath and reeled her emotions back in. Okay, maybe she was being overly sensitive. She counted to two. Three took too long. She might have caught a case by the time she made it to ten. She calmed down some. *Maybe he's like William, not that into her, not that into girls period.*

"I'd get with you in a heartbeat," Leon said, "if I were that kind of guy."

Dakota gave him the side eye.

"Oh, no. That's not what I'm trying to say either." He shook his head. "Damn it, Marie. You got me all mixed up and tongue-tied." He swallowed and took a deep breath. "What I'm trying to say is that I don't want us to turn in for the night." He reached out to take Dakota's hands.

She was a little hesitant but allowed them to rest inside his.

"This is my last night in Vegas. I like you. Hopefully you like me just a little bit or you wouldn't have called me up tonight."

Dakota loosened up and let a smile free.

"Hey, so what do you say we head to the strip? If it's not too late we can see the water show at the Bellagio fountains, take a gondola ride down at the Venetian. Maybe even the hotel I'm staying at has one more outdoor show with those pirates and stuff." He squeezed her hands. "Let's just not let the night end without getting to know each other a little better. Call me crazy, but I don't think it was a coincidence that we ran into each other at the airport, that we're here together tonight. I truly enjoyed your company. You are so down to earth, and I hope this doesn't offend you, but just a little quirky."

Quirky. That was a compliment to Dakota, because that meant that underneath the façade, he was still able to find a true part of her.

"You are one unique individual. It's not every day God blesses someone to encounter a person like you."

"You had me at 'hey,'" Dakota said, mocking one of her favorite movies, *Jerry Maguire*. "You didn't even have to drop the G word: God."

The two laughed.

"So is that a yes? Marie, will you spend the night with me?"

Knowing exactly what Leon meant by spending the night with him, she gladly said, "Yes." But when he lifted her hand, placed it to his sensual lips, and kissed it, her yes just might have changed its intended meaning.

"I feel like I'm in Venice or someplace just like it," Dakota said as she and Leon sat in the gondola as it floated on the waters in the manmade canal inside of the Venetian hotel. It was so late that the outdoor one was closed, but they were just in time to catch the last indoor ride.

It was just beautiful. And when the girl rowing their boat started singing in Italian, Dakota thought she was going to cry. She closed her eyes, and for a moment she forgot she was inside a hotel in Las Vegas. She forgot who she was period. It was no longer about a Dakota versus Marie thing. It was about her just losing herself in the fantasy. But it really wasn't a fantasy. This was real life. Her life. Anyone could call her whatever they wanted. Who she was last week or yesterday didn't matter. Neither did it matter who she was just an hour ago. All that mattered was right now. And right now she was . . . happy.

"Is that a tear I see?" Leon took his index finger and placed it on Dakota's cheek. The tear that slid from her eye landed on the tip of his finger. He slid his finger upward, wiping away the trail the tear had left.

Dakota remained still, her eyes still closed, the entire time. She exhaled as yet another tear fell.

Leon slowly scooted in closer to Dakota. He gently placed his arm around her shoulders and pulled her in to his chest. Dakota just released. So many more tears followed. All tears of joy, none sorrow. None were because of the memories of always being the chubby one when it came to her and Billie, or even her and her clique. Even back in high school she was thick. But through it all, she still tried out for the high school drill team, big legs and all, and made the team. She stayed on the team all four years. She was even voted "Most Spirited" by her senior class. She'd always been blessed with friends who never cared about what size or color she was all the way up to adulthood.

"Girl, I didn't know you were mixed," had been Trice's words to Dakota after she'd met her parents. Trice hadn't cared. Shyla hadn't cared. They'd never asked her once. They'd never been curious about anything other than who she was; not what she was.

"I'm a human being damn it!" Dakota had once snapped off on a college classmate for asking her the infamous "What are you?" question.

"I'm just pretty!" she'd snapped at a guy in the grocery store line for using the "You are pretty to be big," comment, not compliment.

Even Billie, outside of the name calling siblings do when they are younger in heated battles, never got on Dakota about her weight, unlike how adult Toni Braxton did with her adult sister.

The only thing the people who loved Dakota ever cared about when it came to her was just her, and making sure she lived a happy, carefree, fun life.

She couldn't deny that through all their little digs about how she hadn't lived such a life, it had pushed her to do just that while in Vegas.

"You okay?" Leon finally asked.

Dakota opened her eyes, leaving her thoughts. She wiped her tears of joy and complete happiness. She nodded her head as she looked up to face Leon. Staring back at her were eyes that she'd seen before. Trice, Shyla, Billie, her parents; they'd all looked at her with those same eyes. Nothing mattered about Dakota but her. No hidden agenda or thoughts. They didn't look through her or beyond her, just deep within her soul, only yearning to know the person God had created her to be.

Gosh, how she'd love to add his eyes to her collection at home. The more the merrier and it wasn't every day she met someone who deserved to be among those who loved her the most and whom she loved the most in return. But God had made it so that she'd met one more, even if it was just for one night. And Dakota wanted to take advantage of it. So she smiled then placed her head back against Leon's chest and enjoyed her now.

Chapter 13

Dakota stood at the door of her suite looking around the room. What she was looking for only she knew. She'd already scoured the entire place, right down to the shower stall, to the drawers, closet, and under the bed, making sure she wasn't leaving a thing. She surely couldn't have been looking around the room taking in memories. There weren't that many. Most of her memories had definitely been made outside of those four walls, not that anyone who knew her back home would believe. But she knew the truth. She knew the life she'd lived while in Vegas, and she couldn't even hardly believe it, so she surely wasn't going to waste time trying to convince anyone else.

She double checked on top of the nightstand to make sure she'd left housekeeping a tip. She gave the place one last sweep, smiled, then exited the room, heading to the checkout desk.

"How was your stay?" the clerk at the checkout counter asked after Dakota handed him her room key.

"Let's just say that coming back is definitely on my bucket list," Dakota said as the clerk handed her her receipt for the extras she'd purchased such as room service and the items from the hotel stores.

"Were you here for business or pleasure?"

"It was business." Dakota smiled. "But very pleasurable."

"Well, then by all means you must come back and see us, Ms. Smith, for pleasure only."

"Like I said, it's definitely on my bucket list," Dakota assured him as she stuffed the receipt in her purse.

"Good, because you only live once."

Dakota stopped, smiled at the clerk, and said, "Who are you telling?" and with that she shuttled to the airport, heading back to Michigan.

"Sister!" Billie exclaimed as soon as she saw Dakota approach the baggage claim where she'd been waiting for her.

"Billie." Dakota put down her carry-on and hugged her sister. "Thank you for coming to pick me up from the airport."

"Of course." Billie grabbed Dakota's suitcase by the handle. "I saw your suitcase come around the bend, so I grabbed it. And telling by its weight, you got some shopping done. I hope you bought me something. And not some stupid airport souvenir."

Dakota laughed. "Well, what had happened was . . ."

Billie rolled her eyes up in her head already knowing she wasn't about to like what Dakota had to say.

"I meant to pick up everyone something while I was shopping at the mall, but it totally slipped my mind."

Billie frowned. "So you didn't bring us back nothing?"

"Of course I did: some stupid airport souvenirs." Dakota busted out laughing at the distorted face Billie was making. "Sorry. I didn't want to have to pay an arm and a leg for those ridiculous things either."

"Well, thank goodness you won five thousand dollars. You can just give me some of that." Billie held her hand out. "Yep, Dad told me. I talked to you how many times, and you kept that from me. Umm, hmmm. I see how you are."

"Girl, come on." Dakota picked up her carry-on. Billie pulled her sister's suitcase and the two headed toward the exit so they could walk over to the garage that Billie had parked in.

"So tell me. What was Vegas like? Did you follow my advice and let your hair down and live a little?" Billie asked as soon as they stepped out of the airport.

Dakota looked over at Billie and wagged her finger in her sister's face. "Oh, no you don't. Remember it's like you said: what goes on in Vegas stays in Vegas. And I did just that: left it all behind me." Dakota stuck her tongue out at her sister.

"Oh goodness!" Dakota felt like she'd run into a brick wall. Instead it was a man who had been walking in front of her. Obviously while Dakota was teasing her sister, the man in front of her had halted his steps for some reason.

"I'm so sorry," Dakota apologized to the gentleman.

He turned around with his mouth opened prepared to speak. His words got caught. He quickly recovered them though. "Marie?"

"Leon!" Dakota replied in shock.

Guess not everything had stayed in Vegas after all.

ORDER FORM
URBAN BOOKS, LLC
97 N18th Street
Wyandanch, NY 11798

Name (please print):_____

Address: _____

City/State: _____

Zip: _____

QTY	TITLES	PRICE

Shipping and handling: add $3.50 for 1st book, then $1.75 for each additional book.
Please send a check payable to:
    Urban Books, LLC
Please allow 4-6 weeks for delivery